"You aren't going to come to church with us, are you?"

The second the question was out of her mouth, she bit down on the inside of her cheek. She'd never confronted someone about not attending church. She didn't confront anyone about anything, if possible.

Chance's gaze narrowed on her face, every line in his body rigid. "I need to get settled in."

Tanya knew from the expression on her new tenant's handsome face that any further discussion was unwelcome. "I'm sorry I brought up the subject. I just assumed you believed."

"Because I'm friends with Samuel?"

She nodded.

"I guess Samuel would say I'm the lost sheep he's trying to bring back to the fold."

THE LADIES OF SWEETWATER LAKE:
Like a wedding ring, this circle
of friends is never ending

MARGARET DALEY

feels she has been blessed. She has been married more than thirty years to her husband, Mike, whom she met in college. He is a terrific support and her best friend. They have one son, Shaun. Margaret has been writing for many years and loves to tell a story. When she was a little girl, she would play with her dolls and make up stories about their lives. Now she writes these stories down. She especially enjoys weaving stories about families and how faith in God can sustain a person when things get tough. When she isn't writing, she is fortunate to be a teacher for students with special needs. Margaret has taught for over twenty years and loves working with her students. She has also been a Special Olympics coach and participated in many sports with her students.

MARGARET DALEY

Tidings of Joy

Steeple Hill®

Published by Steeple Hill Books™

STEEPLE HILL BOOKS

Steeple
Hill®

ISBN-13: 978-0-373-81283-7
ISBN-10: 0-373-81283-3

TIDINGS OF JOY

Copyright © 2006 by Margaret Daley

www.SteepleHill.com

Printed in U.S.A.

And ye now therefore have sorrow: but I will see you again, and your heart shall rejoice, and your joy no man taketh from you.
—*John* 16:22

To my family—I love you

Chapter One

Chance Taylor stepped off the bus and surveyed the town, which was nothing like where he'd spent the past two years. Yet, for a few seconds he fought the overwhelming urge to get back on the bus. Because no matter how much he wanted to, he couldn't. Not until he'd paid his debt.

The bus pulled away from the curb, leaving him behind. No escape now. The beating of his heart kicked up a notch. Chance glanced up and down the street. Sweetwater. It was exactly as Tom Bolton had described it. Quaint stores lined its Main Street. A row of Bradford pear trees down both sides of the road offered shade in the heat of summer. Even though it was the end of September, the hot air caused sweat to pop out on his forehead.

He closed his eyes to the vivid colors spread out before him—a red sign above a door, yellow pansies about the base of the trees along the street. He'd lived in a world he'd thought of as black-and-white. Now every hue of the rainbow bombarded him from all sides. Opening his eyes to the new world around him, he wiped the sweat from his brow with the back of his hand, then grabbed the one duffel bag with all his earthly possessions and strode toward Alice's Café.

Inside he scanned the diners, all engrossed in their food and conversation. People doing normal, everyday things with no idea how their life could change in a split second. But he knew.

Drawing in a deep breath, Chance took a moment to compose himself. Again the question flashed across his mind: why had he come to Sweetwater? Surely there was a better place, one he could get lost in. New York City. Chicago. Even Louisville would have been better than this small town, where according to Tom, everyone watched out for each other. He didn't want that. Nosy neighbors had led to his destruction in the past. But Sweetwater was the only place where he could fulfill his promise to himself. He was stuck here for the time being, but once he had paid his debt, he would leave as fast as a bus could take him out of town.

Chance saw Samuel Morgan in the back booth and headed toward him. Aware of a few glances thrown his way, Chance hurried over, placed his duffel bag on the floor, then slid in across from Samuel, his back to the other diners.

Samuel grinned. "I didn't think you'd come."

"I said I would. About the only thing I have left is my word."

"Tom's death wasn't your fault. He made his choice."

"I have a chance to return a favor. I intend to. That's the least I can do."

A waitress with a pencil behind her left ear paused near Samuel and dug into her apron pocket for a pad.

"Want something to eat?" Samuel asked.

Chance shook his head, aware of the open curiosity in the older woman's gaze. His stomach tightened. He should be used to people watching him, having spent the past few years with no right to any privacy. But he wasn't. All he wanted when he was through with Sweetwater was to find a quiet corner of the world where he could put his life back together.

"Alice, I'll take another cup of coffee." Samuel pushed his mug toward the edge of the table.

"Sure, Reverend. Be right back."

After Alice refilled Samuel's coffee and left,

he said, "Your timing couldn't be better. Tanya Bolton has just converted the space over her garage into an apartment. She's looking for a tenant and you need a place to stay. It's perfect."

Something in the reverend's expression alerted Chance that there was more to it. "You wouldn't have anything to do with Tom's wife having an apartment, now would you?"

Samuel's grin reached deep into his eyes. "I did mention it would be a great way for her to make some extra money. She took the suggestion and ran with it."

"I can't see the lady renting to an ex-con."

"You aren't an ex-con. Your conviction was overturned because you were innocent. The police have the right guy in jail now."

The horror of the past few years threatened to deluge Chance with all the memories he desperately needed to forget. He refused to let them intrude, shoving them back into the dark corner of his mind. He didn't have the emotional strength to return to the past. His wounds ran deep, to his very soul. "It doesn't change the fact that I spent two years in prison. When she finds that out…" He couldn't finish his sentence, the words clogging his throat. The knot in his stomach grew.

Suddenly he pictured a man he'd thought was

a good friend, and his expression when Chance had seen him last week in Louisville. Fear had flitted across his so-called friend's features before he could mask his reaction to seeing Chance. Although in the eyes of the law he had been exonerated, he had seen the doubt in the man's gaze. *Did they have the right guy this time?*

Samuel leaned toward Chance and said in a low tone, "I'm not telling Tanya anything about your recent past. I'll leave that for you to tell when you feel ready. But I am going to vouch for you. I know you're a good, honest man, and what you've come to Sweetwater to do is important to you."

Chance thought about being so near Tom's wife on a daily basis. He wasn't sure he could handle it, the constant reminder that he owed his life to Tom. "Is there anywhere else I can rent a room?"

"Probably. But not as convenient, that is if you really want to help Tanya. Or are you here to hide?"

Samuel's question pierced through the layers of protection Chance used to shield himself from others. If he was smart, he would leave and do exactly that.

"Look you don't have any way of getting

around except walking, and Tanya's house is close to downtown so you can get just about any place you'll need to go from that apartment."

Chance held up his hand. "Okay, Reverend. You've convinced me. I'll see the lady about it."

Samuel took a long sip of his coffee. "Good. I also have lined up the interview with Nick Blackburn for that job I told you about when we spoke last week on the phone. He's looking for an assistant to help him with the part of his company he's moved to Sweetwater. Still interested?"

"I need a job while I live here, so yes, I'm still interested. What does Mr. Blackburn know about me?"

"That you are a friend of mine, that's all."

"I'll have to tell him where I've been."

"Yeah, I know, but it needs to come from you. Nick will respect that." Samuel sipped his coffee.

"When's the interview?"

"Nine o'clock tomorrow morning. His office is two blocks down on Main. The brand-new, seven-story tall redbrick building. You probably saw it coming into town on the bus."

"Yeah. He works Saturdays?" Everything was moving so fast. Was he ready to plunge back into the world of big business? Once that had been his life. Once he'd worked long hours to get ahead at his job. Now he wished he had that time back, that he'd spent it with the family he no longer had.

"Sometimes. Usually he spends his weekends with his family, but he knew you were arriving today and decided to do it tomorrow. He said something about having to be in Chicago early next week."

"I've heard of Blackburn Industries. I didn't realize he'd moved his corporate offices from Chicago to Sweetwater."

Samuel shrugged. "Love is a strong motivator. His wife is from here." Samuel finished his cup of coffee. "I'll drive you over to Tanya's."

"No, I need to do this on my own. You can call her and give her a reference so she'll open the door, but the rest will have to be up to me."

"Fine, but Chance, you aren't alone in this world. I told you that in prison and I'm telling you that now."

"I know. I know, Reverend. God is with me. He stood by me while I watched my family taken from me and while I was on trial. He was there with me in prison when I was fighting for my life." Chance saw the disappointment in Samuel's eyes that his sarcastic words had caused.

"I know how you feel, but you didn't give Him a chance to be with you."

Chance slipped from the booth. He didn't want to hear it. Samuel knew how he felt about the Lord who had abandoned him in his time of need. They'd even had a discussion about it when Samuel had come to the prison to minister to the inmates. "How do I get to Tanya Bolton's house?"

Samuel wrote an address on a napkin and handed it to him. "Go three blocks north on Main to Second, then go five blocks east on Second and that's Berryhill Road. Sure you don't want me to at least drop you off?"

"No, the exercise will be good for me." Chance turned from the booth and headed for the door. The very act of going anywhere he wanted was precious to him. He would never take freedom of movement for granted again.

Outside he relished the warmth of the sun on his face, the fresh air, laced with newly mowed grass and grilled meat from a barbecue restaurant on the next block. A slender man dressed in a suit passed him on the sidewalk and nodded a greeting. Automatically Chance returned it with his own nod. The sudden realization that for the next few months he would be thrust into the middle of life in a small town sent panic bolting through him. He'd grown up in a small town and knew that little was a secret for long. He didn't want to see the doubt and possibly even fear in the eyes of the residents of Sweetwater when they learned he'd been in prison.

"I've got the sign out in front and I've advertised in the paper. Now all I need is someone to rent the apartment over the garage," Tanya Bolton said as she switched the cordless phone to her other ear.

"You did such a nice job fixing the place up. I don't think you'll have any trouble finding a tenant."

"I hope you're right, Zoey, because I need the money. Having a teenage daughter who's growing out of all her clothes is expensive."

"Will I see you at Alice's Café tomorrow?"

"Of course. I wouldn't miss our Saturday get-together." Tanya lowered her voice, cupping the mouthpiece closer to her. "I don't know if I would have made it without you, Darcy, Beth and Jesse. You know I'll be there."

"See you tomorrow," Zoey Witherspoon said as a beep sounded, indicating another call on the line.

Tanya pushed a button. "Hello?"

"This is Samuel. I'm glad you're home, Tanya. I've got a friend coming over right now to see your apartment. He's going to be here for a while and needs a place to stay."

"A tenant! I was just talking to Zoey about not having shown the apartment to anyone yet."

"Then this is your lucky day. He'll be a great tenant. His name is Chance Taylor."

The sound of the doorbell ringing drew Tanya's attention. She walked toward the front door with the cordless phone still in her hand and noticed through the frosted glass a large man on her porch. "Looks like he's here. Thanks, Samuel. I really appreciate the referral." She laid the phone on the table in the small foyer, then hurriedly opened the door.

Before her stood a man several inches over six feet tall with broad shoulders, a narrow waist and muscular arms. His large presence dwarfed her small porch and blocked her doorway. Her gaze flew to his face, taking in his hard, square jaw, his nose that had been broken once, his vivid blue eyes and his short black hair. All his features came together in a pleasing countenance with just a hint of sadness in it. Surprised by that thought, Tanya wasn't sure where the impression came from.

His neutral expression evolved into a half grin. "Tanya Bolton?"

His presence filled her vision. "Yes," she

managed to say, stunned by how overpowering Samuel's friend was.

"I'm Chance Taylor. Samuel was supposed to call you about me. I'd like to rent your apartment."

The deep, baritone of his voice flowed over her, smooth like a river of honey. Slowly his dark blue eyes lit with a gleam like periwinkles basking in the sunlight. Then his mouth lifted in a full grin, causing dimples to appear in both cheeks.

"Is it still for rent?"

She nodded, for some reason her voice still unable to work properly.

"How much?"

She mentally shook herself out of her daze. This was business. "Three hundred a month plus utilities."

He dug into the front pocket of his black jeans and withdrew a wad of cash. After peeling off three one hundred dollar bills, crisp and new, he handed them to her.

She peered at the money, thinking of all the bills she needed to pay. Then common sense prevailed. "I don't want to take your money until you've seen the apartment."

"I'm not choosy about where I stay."

"The apartment is open. It's above the detached garage at the side of the house. Why don't you go and take a look at it? I wouldn't feel right if you didn't do that. I'll be along in a moment."

After repocketing his money, he tipped his head toward her. "I'll do that, Mrs. Bolton."

She watched him descend the steps with duffel bag in hand, then head for the garage. When he disappeared from view, she went into the kitchen and grabbed the lease that Beth had insisted she needed a tenant to sign and left the house by the back door.

Her daughter would be home from school in half an hour, and she hoped to have this all settled by then. After she crossed the driveway, she climbed the stairs to the apartment over the garage at the side of the house. The door stood ajar.

Inside Chance slowly turned in a full circle, surveying the place, no expression on his face. When he saw her, he stopped, one corner of his mouth hitched in a half grin, dimpling one cheek. She was beginning to wonder if that was his trademark.

"This is nice."

His compliment caused a catch in her throat. She'd worked hard on the apartment with some help from her friends and was proud of what she'd accomplished on a limited budget. "Thanks."

He faced her, his large presence filling the small two-room apartment—much like her porch—his shoulders set in a taut line, his arms straight at his sides. His gaze lit upon the paper she held in her hand. "Do you want me to sign a lease?"

"Yes. This is for six months."

"I don't know how long I'll be here. I've got an interview with Nick Blackburn about a job, but nothing's definite."

Tanya glanced at the standard lease and folded it several times. "Then we won't use the lease. Where did you come from?"

"Louisville."

"Why did you come to Sweetwater? Because of the possibility of a job with Nick?"

"No, actually Samuel has always talked so highly of Sweetwater that I decided to come pay him and the town a visit. He knew I was looking for a job and mentioned the one with Blackburn Industries." Again Chance withdrew the wad of money from his pocket and unrolled it. Covering the short distance between them, he thrust the rent toward her. "Three hundred. Do you require a deposit?"

Deposit? Tanya bit her lower lip. She hadn't thought about that. Having never been a landlord before, she realized how new this all was to her. "I guess a hundred. That should cover minor damages if there are any."

"There won't be."

"Not from what Samuel says. He basically told me I couldn't go wrong with you being my tenant."

Chance glanced away for a few seconds as if embarrassed by what Samuel had said. Clearing his throat, he returned his attention to her. "Samuel does have a way about him." He gave her the money for the deposit, then immediately stepped back as though he was uncomfortable getting too near her. He looked toward the kitchen area in one corner with a two-burner stove, a sink and a small refrigerator. "Can you give me directions to the nearest grocery store?"

Tanya thought of the bare kitchen and blurted out, "Why don't you have dinner with me and my daughter tonight? That's the least I can do for someone new to Sweetwater and a friend of Samuel's."

Chance plunged his fingers through his black hair, then massaged the back of his neck. "I don't want you to go to any trouble, Mrs. Bolton."

"My name is Tanya and it isn't any trouble. I have to warn you, though, it won't be anything fancy."

"I'm not used to fancy."

The tight edge to his words made her blink in surprise. "Well, then you'll fit right in. Sweetwater's pretty laid-back. We only have one expensive restaurant that I've never seen the inside of."

"What time is dinner?"

Tanya checked her watch and realized that Crystal would be home from school soon. "Give me a couple of hours. Say six." She backed toward the door, a sudden, awkward silence electrifying the air. "See you then."

Out on the landing she breathed deeply. Chance Taylor wasn't a chatty person. She would have to quiz Samuel about him. For some reason she didn't think her new tenant would tell her much about himself. The click of the door closing behind her penetrated her thoughts. She couldn't shake the feeling his life hadn't been easy. The sight of the school bus coming down the street sent Tanya hurrying down the stairs.

Even though Crystal was fifteen now and a freshman in high school, when her job allowed her, Tanya liked to be there when her daughter came home from school, especially lately. Something was bothering Crystal and her daughter wouldn't talk to her about it. Maybe today Crystal would say something that would reveal what was going on. She rounded the side of the garage when the bus stopped and the driver descended the steps to man the lift.

While Crystal powered her wheelchair up the driveway, the small school bus drove away. If the frown on her daughter's face was any indication, today had not been a good one. Tanya sighed and met Crystal halfway.

"We have a tenant for the apartment," Tanya said, forcing a light tone into her voice to cover the apprehension her child's expression raised.

Her daughter didn't say a word. She maneuvered the wheelchair around Tanya and kept going toward the ramp at the back of the house. Tanya followed, trying to decide how to approach Crystal about what was happening at school. This year when she had begun at Sweetwater High, she'd quickly started trying to get out of going, even to the point of making up things that were wrong with her. Tanya had talked with her teachers, but no one knew what was going on. She had seen her usually happy, even-tempered child become someone else, someone who was angry and resentful. Was it the typical teenager angst of going through puberty? Or was it something else? Had Crystal's father's death finally manifested itself in her troubled behavior? Tom had died almost five months ago, and their daughter had gone through the usual grief associated with death but had seemed all right as her summer vacation had come to an end. Now Tanya didn't know. Maybe Crystal had suppressed her true feelings.

In the kitchen Tanya called out to Crystal before she wheeled herself through the doorway into the hall, "Our new tenant is joining us for dinner."

Crystal continued to remain quiet as she disappeared from view. Perplexed, Tanya stared at the empty doorway, wondering if Zoey, a high school counselor, or Beth Morgan, Crystal's English teacher, knew what was going on with her daughter at school. She made a mental note to call her friends later to see if anything had happened today to warrant this sullen demeanor.

Chance descended the stairs to his apartment over the garage and headed across the yard toward the back door. He noticed the ramp off the deck and remembered Tom talking about his teenage daughter who was in a wheelchair. Until he had seen the ramp, however, he hadn't really thought about the implication of having a child who was physically disabled or the fact that he would be eating with a young girl who would only be a year or two older than the age his own daughter would have been if she had lived.

He stopped his progress toward the deck, indecision stiffening his body. He'd seen plenty of teenagers since his daughter's…death. Surely he could handle an hour in the same room with Tanya's child. How difficult could it be?

Chance discovered a few minutes later just how hard it would be when Crystal opened the door to his knock, a smile on her thin face, a black Lab standing beside her. He sucked in a sharp breath and held it. Staring up at him with open interest was a young girl who had dark brown hair and hazel eyes, so very reminiscent of his daughter's. She even had a sprinkle of freckles on her small upturned nose as Haley had.

He cleared away the huge knot in his throat and struggled against the urge to run as far away as he could. His legs refused to move forward into the house even though Tanya's daughter opened the door wider for him.

"Come in before all the insects do," Tanya said, approaching them.

He shook off the panic beginning to swell in his chest and shuffled into the kitchen. Turning to shut the back door, he took a few precious seconds to compose his reeling emotions at the sharp reminder of what he'd lost. When he pivoted back toward the pair, his feelings were tamped down beneath all the defensive layers he'd created over the past few years. Under closer inspection of Tom's daughter, he saw no real similarities between Haley and her, other than their coloring.

If he was going to repay the debt, he had no choice but to learn to deal with the teenager—and the mother. *I can do this,* he told himself and forced a smile to his lips. "I'm Chance, the new tenant," he said to Crystal, realizing he was probably stating the obvious.

The teenager's smile grew. "I'm Crystal. Welcome to Sweetwater."

"Thanks." He inhaled the aroma of ground beef that peppered the air. "It smells wonderful. What are we having?"

"As I told you earlier, nothing fancy. Just tacos. I hope you like Mexican food. Crystal and I love it." Tanya gestured toward the counter. "Everyone's going to put their own together."

"I like anything I don't have to cook." He took another few steps farther into the kitchen, committing himself to spending some time with his landlady and her daughter.

Tanya handed him a plate with big yellow and blue flowers painted on it. "You don't cook then?"

"Not unless you call heating up a can of spaghetti cooking."

Crystal giggled, patting her dog. "Even I can do that."

"My daughter's taking a Foods and Nutrition class this year. Hopefully she'll learn more than heating up what's in a can."

Chance noticed the instant school was mentioned that Crystal's cheerful expression vanished and the young girl dropped her head, her attention glued to her lap. Did she struggle with schoolwork? He made a note to find out. Maybe he could help her with her homework, then he would be one step closer to being able to leave Sweetwater, to appeasing his guilt.

"You go first." Tanya swept her arm across her body, indicating he prepare his tacos.

Chance took two large empty shells and filled them with the meat sauce, cheese, lettuce and diced tomatoes. His mouth watered in anticipation of his first home-cooked meal in years. After he doused his tacos with chunky salsa, he made his way to the round oak table in the alcove with three large windows overlooking the deck and backyard.

He sat at one of the places already set with

utensils, a blue linen napkin and a glass with ice in it. When he noticed a pitcher on the table, he poured himself some tea, then doctored it with several scoops of sugar.

Crystal positioned herself next to him and put her plate on her yellow place mat. "Mom said you're from Louisville. I went there once, when I was nine, and took a riverboat up the Ohio River."

As Tanya settled into the chair across from him, Chance said to Crystal, "I've never ridden on a riverboat. Did you like it?"

"Yeah! I'd like to take one all the way to New Orleans. I've never been to New Orleans. I haven't seen very many places." She glanced down at her wheelchair, then fixed her large hazel eyes on him as though that explained why she didn't go places.

A tightness constricted his chest. He couldn't imagine being confined to a wheelchair, every little bump in the terrain an obstacle, not free to move about as you wanted. He knew about that and had hated every second of his confinement. "You'll have time," he finally said, feeling a connection between him and Crystal that went beyond her father.

"That's what Mom says."

"I promised her a trip when she graduates

from high school." Tanya poured tea for herself and her daughter. "She'll get to pick where, depending on my budget."

"Mom's got a saving account for the trip at the bank where she works."

"That's a good plan." After he picked up his taco carefully so as not to make a mess, he took a big bite, relishing the spicy meat sauce. "Mmm. This is good."

Tanya smiled. "Thanks."

She and Crystal bowed their heads while Tanya said a prayer.

When she glanced up at Chance, he'd put his taco back on his plate, a look of unease in his expression. "I don't have the time to cook like I want to, but I do enjoy getting into the kitchen when I can," she said, hoping to make him feel comfortable.

"I'm glad you invited me." Chance caught her gaze and held it for a long moment. He realized he meant what he had just said. The warmth emanating from both the mother and daughter spoke to a part of him that he thought had died in prison.

Finally Tanya dropped her regard and ran her finger around the rim of her glass. "What kind of job are you applying for with Nick?"

"As an assistant for his office in Sweetwater."

"Nick said something to me about expanding his company's presence in Sweetwater. I guess this must be the beginning. Since he and Jesse got married, I know he doesn't like to travel to Chicago as much as he used to. What have you done before?"

Tension knifed through Chance. He should have expected questions about his past. That was the last thing he wanted to discuss. "I was a financial advisor."

"Was? Not anymore?"

"I'm looking for something different. That's why this assistant's job interests me." That and the fact Samuel paved the way for him with Nick Blackburn. But even with Samuel's reference, the job wasn't a sure thing. He would have to convince Mr. Blackburn he could do the work, definitely a step down from what he'd done in the past where he'd had his own assistant.

"What happens if you don't get the job?"

"I'm still staying for a while. I'll just look for another one," he quickly said to ease the worry he heard in her voice.

He needed the conversation focused on someone else. Angling around toward Crystal, he asked, "Besides Foods and Nutrition, what else are you taking?"

The teenager downed a swallow of tea. "I'm

taking the usual—U.S. history, English, algebra and biology. I'm also in the girls' choir."

"In high school I was in the show choir. I enjoyed it." Chance felt Tanya's puzzled gaze on him and shifted in his chair, feeling uncomfortable under her scrutiny as though she could see into his heart and soul. Their emptiness wasn't something he wanted exposed to the world. He busied himself by taking another bite.

"I sing in the choir at church. We can always use another man to sing."

He heard Tanya's words of encouragement and gritted his teeth so hard that pain streaked down his neck. Church. Religion. God wasn't for him. He'd believed once, and his whole life, his family, had been taken away from him. He stuffed the rest of the taco into his mouth and occupied himself with chewing—slowly. Averting his gaze, he stared out the window at the backyard and hoped the woman didn't pursue the topic of conversation.

"I thought about auditioning for the show choir, but I didn't. I can't dance very well in this thing," Crystal slapped the arm of her wheelchair, "and you have to be able to sing *and* dance to be in it. If I can't do it right, I don't want to do it at all."

The teenager's words cut through the tension gripping Chance. He looked back at her and managed to smile, hearing the need in the child's voice that twisted his heart. "Besides singing, what else do you like to do?"

"I like to draw."

"Why aren't you taking art in school?"

"I can't take everything. I'll probably take it next year." Crystal shrugged. "Besides, Mom's teaching me. She's very good."

Chance swung his attention to Tanya who looked away when his gaze fell on her. "What do you like to draw?"

A hint of red tinged her cheeks. "People mostly."

"Portraits?"

"Nothing formal like that."

"I'd love to see your work sometime."

Tanya started to say something when Crystal chimed in, "I'll go get her sketchbook. It's in the dining room." She backed up her wheelchair, made a one-hundred-eighty-degree turn, and headed for the door with her service dog following.

"I get the impression you don't show many people your drawings."

She shook her head, swallowing hard. "I'm not very good. I draw for myself."

When Crystal came back into the kitchen with the sketchbook in her lap, Chance wanted to make Tanya feel at ease so he said, "I don't want to intrude on—"

"Mom, doesn't think she's good. I do. Here, see for yourself." Crystal opened the book and showed Chance.

He wasn't sure what to expect after Tanya's reluctant reaction, but what he saw was an exquisite portrait of Crystal sketching something. The drawing captured the teenager's love for art in the detailed expression on her face. The pen-and-ink picture was as good as any professional artist would have done. "I'm impressed, Tanya. This is beautiful."

"You think so?"

All the woman's doubts were evident in her wrinkled forehead, the hesitant expression in her eyes and the hidden hope that he might really be telling her the truth. As before it was important to Chance to make Tanya feel comfortable. "Yes. I'm honored to have seen this. You should show your drawings more often."

Tanya straightened in her chair, her head cocked. "Samuel tried to get me to have one in the Fourth of July auction this year at church. I told him I would donate my time or something else."

Chance captured Tanya's regard. "Next year take him up on the offer."

She slid her gaze away and started gathering up her plate and utensils. "I'll think about it."

"Which means she won't do it," Crystal interjected and put her dishes in her lap then wheeled herself toward the sink.

Chance followed them with his place setting. "I hope you'll let me help you clean up after being gracious enough to invite me to dinner. I might not cook very well, but I can rinse and put them in the dishwasher."

"Yeah, Mom. Let him."

Tanya laughed. "You're agreeing because you'll get out of your part of cleaning up."

"I've got homework to do."

"On Friday night?"

Crystal lifted her shoulders. "What else is there to do?"

"Fine." Tanya watched her frowning daughter and the black Lab disappear into the hallway. "Something's bothering her. I wish she would tell me."

"She's what, fifteen, sixteen?"

"Fifteen."

"Did you tell your mother what was going on with you at that age?"

"Good point. But still we've been through a

lot. I…" Her voice quavering, Tanya twisted away so her face was hidden as she stacked the dishes into the sink and turned on the water.

Chance heard the thickness lacing each word and wished he could help her. But he discovered that helping her was going to be harder than he'd thought. Actually he'd had no plan in mind other than to assist Tom's family. But how? Maybe he could reach Crystal. He had to try something or he would never be able to get on with his life—what was left of it.

Tanya handed him the first plate to put in the dishwasher. "You should come hear us sing in the choir at church this Sunday. As I'm sure you're aware, Samuel gives great sermons."

Chance gripped the glass she passed to him. "I'll think about it."

Chapter Two

Chance's clipped words caused Tanya to step back, strained uneasiness pulsating between them. She got the distinct impression thinking was all he would do about going to church.

Without really contemplating what she was saying, she asked, "You aren't going to come, are you?" The second the question was out of her mouth, she bit down on the inside of her cheek. She'd never confronted someone about not attending church. She didn't confront anyone about anything, if possible.

His gaze narrowed on her face, every line in his body rigid. "I need to get settled in."

By his tight tone, evasive answer and clenched jaw, Tanya knew that any further discussion was unwelcome. "I'm sorry I brought up the subject. I just assumed you believed."

"Because I'm friends with Samuel?"

She nodded.

"I guess Samuel would say I'm the lost sheep he's trying to bring back to the fold."

"So you've heard him speak before?"

"Yeah. But it's not going to change how I feel. Simply put, God wasn't there for me when I needed Him the most."

His statement piqued her curiosity and made her wonder even more about Chance Taylor's past. She handed him another dish and let the silence lengthen while she decided how to proceed with the conversation when tension crowded the space between them. "What happened?" She realized she was pushing when she never pushed.

"Nothing I want to revisit."

His answer hadn't surprised her. She didn't think he shared willingly much of himself with anyone. She'd seen that same defensive mechanism in Tom, especially after the riding accident that had left Crystal paralyzed. "You said you were a financial advisor. I wish I had a knack for figures. My budget's in a terrible mess. I work at a bank, but finances aren't my strong suit." There, that should be a safe enough subject for conversation.

"What do you do?"

"I started out as a receptionist, but I'm a teller now. I can count money, just not manage my own very well. There never seems to be enough to go around. I'm still paying off Crystal's medical expenses." And her deceased ex-husband's lawyer's bill, she added silently, not wanting to go into what happened with Tom. How do you explain to a person you just met that your husband was sent to prison for burning barns in retaliation for their daughter's accident?

"When was the last time you redid your budget?"

"I don't exactly have one that's written down. I pay the most important bills first, then as much as I can on the ones left. That's the extent of my budget. Some months I do better than others." She could remember her spending spree several years back where she had bought unnecessary items—expensive clothing, inessential furniture. Thankfully she had been able to take a lot of them back—but not all. She'd finally paid off those bills a few months ago. So long as she stayed on the medication she took for manic depression, she shouldn't get herself into a bind like that again. She couldn't afford to.

After he put the last glass on the top rack, Chance closed the dishwasher. "Maybe I can help you with that."

"Would you? That would be great! If the job with Nick doesn't work out, I may be able to help you find one. I can ask around." There was something about Chance that drew her to him. She wanted to help him, especially in light of him offering to assist her with her budget.

He frowned, rubbing his hand along the back of his neck. "You don't—"

"Mom, I'm going out on the deck to do my homework. Now that the sun's going down behind the trees, it's cooler outside." With a book and pad in her lap, Crystal wheeled herself toward the back door.

Chance hurried to open it before her daughter could. "What subject are you working on?"

"English. I have an essay to write. I do my best thinking outside."

"So do I."

When Crystal was out on the deck, Chance turned toward Tanya. "I'd better go. It's been a long day, and tomorrow I have that job interview, then I need to buy some supplies."

"Pretty much whatever you need can be found on Main Street or right off it. There's a grocery store four blocks from here on Third Avenue."

"Is that right after Second?"

"Yep."

"Then I think I can find it on my walk," he said with a smile.

"You don't have a car?"

"No, I came on the bus."

"I'm going to Alice's Café tomorrow at ten. What time is your interview?"

"Nine."

"I can give you a lift, if you'd like. I have a few errands I need to run before I meet my friends."

"Thanks, but I can walk. I like the exercise."

His half grin appeared, and for a few seconds Tanya's heart responded by quickening its beat. Her physical reaction took her by surprise. After her ordeal with Tom, men hadn't interested her—until now.

Chance left and stopped next to Crystal to say a few words to her, then proceeded toward the detached garage at the side of the house. Tanya came out onto the deck and watched him. While he'd talked with her daughter, Tanya had glimpsed a vulnerability leaking into his expression. He had managed to cover it quickly, but she had seen it.

"What do you think of our new tenant?" Tanya asked when she noticed her daughter watching her staring at Chance.

"What do *you* think?"

"He seems nice. Kinda lonely."

"Yeah."

"What did he say to you?"

Crystal tilted her head, screwing up her face into a quizzical expression. "He offered to tutor me in math if I needed it."

Tanya laughed. "Did you tell him you had a ninety-eight in Algebra I and that you're taking Algebra II?"

She nodded. "I wonder why he offered."

"Did you ask him?"

"He left before I could. Maybe I will tomorrow."

"Speaking of tomorrow, I'd better get a load of laundry done tonight or neither of us will have anything to wear."

When Tanya entered the kitchen, her gaze fell on the table where Chance had sat for dinner. He was a puzzle. And one of her favorite things to do was put together jigsaw puzzles, the more pieces the better. She had a feeling there were a lot of pieces to Chance Taylor.

"Have a seat." Nick Blackburn indicated a brown leather chair in front of his large desk.

Chance quickly scanned the spacious office as he sat. The rich walnut tones of the furniture with a navy-and-brown color scheme lent a refined elegance to the room. He'd been in many offices that conveyed power and wealth. This one ranked near the top.

Mr. Blackburn perused the application Chance had filled out, and he knew the second the man read about his time spent in the state penitentiary. To give Mr. Blackburn credit, he finished the application before he glanced up at Chance and asked, "What did you do time for?"

"Murder."

The man's eyes widened slightly before he put the paper down, a bland expression veiling his curiosity. "You only served two years?"

"My conviction was overturned when the real murderer was apprehended last month."

"So you served two years for a crime you didn't commit."

Even though it really wasn't a question, Chance said, "Yes."

"That's where you met Samuel?"

"Yes, sir. He took an interest in me and we became friends."

"You know you're overqualified for this job. You have an MBA from Harvard. You've worked for several top money-managing companies in the country and were on the fast track."

"Were is the operative word here. That was in my past. Besides—" Chance grinned

"—Blackburn Industries is well respected and a multimillion dollar business. I consider this job an opportunity to do something different."

"Because you don't see people letting you manage their money after spending time in prison?"

Chance leaned forward. "To be frank, I don't want to be reminded of the life I once had. I need to start over in something totally different. What are the duties of the job?"

After Mr. Blackburn listed them for Chance, the man said, "Do you think you can handle those?"

In his sleep, Chance thought and nodded.

"There will be some traveling to my Chicago office. The dress is casual here but not in Chicago."

"I understand."

Nick Blackburn pushed back his chair and stood. Offering Chance his hand, he said, "Then you've got yourself a job. I've never known Samuel to be wrong about a person, and he thinks you can do this job."

"When do I start, Mr. Blackburn?"

"It's Nick, and you can start Wednesday morning when I get back from Chicago. Be here at nine and I'll show you around and introduce you to the staff here in Sweetwater."

A few minutes later as Chance left the building, he couldn't resist turning his face to the sun, relishing its warmth as it bathed him. He would never tire of doing that.

He had a job. That was one worry taken care of. Now all he had to figure out was how to be there for Tanya and Crystal without them knowing why. After spending time with them the night before, he wasn't sure he wanted them ever to know his involvement in Tom's death.

"Okay, you have to tell us about the guy renting your apartment." Jesse scooted over in the booth at Alice's Café to allow Tanya to slide in beside her. "We've all been waiting with bated breath."

"Jesse Blackburn, don't you get any ideas. No matchmaking! He's only my tenant. Just passing through." Taking a sip of her coffee, Tanya looked around the group and added, "How did you know I have a man renting my garage apartment?"

Beth Morgan grinned. "Samuel told me. Do you think there are any secrets among us after all these years?"

"What else did your husband say?" Tanya thought about all she wanted to know concerning her tenant, especially what or who was responsible for the pain behind his half smile that never quite reached his eyes. She hadn't slept much the night before, her mind insisting on playing through all kinds of scenarios.

"Not much. Samuel just told me you rented your apartment to Chance Taylor, a friend from his past. You know my husband. He doesn't say much about a person he knows. He always likes people to make up their own mind. So spill the beans. What's he look like?"

An image of the first time she had seen Chance on her porch flashed into Tanya's mind. Even from the beginning she'd been drawn to his eyes where she'd seen a shadow of sadness in their depths. "He's very tall, dark hair, blue eyes, nice build, probably in his late thirties. He had an interview this morning with Nick about the assistant's job."

Surprise widened Jesse's eyes. "He did and Nick didn't tell me."

"This isn't a secretarial-type position, is it?" Zoey Witherspoon asked.

Jesse shook her head. "More like Nick's right hand. Someone he can train to take over part of his duties that demand he travel to Chicago."

"Chance's background is in finance so he should be qualified," Tanya said, glad she knew at least that much about her new tenant.

With her elbow on the table, Darcy Markham rested her chin in her palm. "Mmm. He sounds promising."

"Hey, you're married to a very nice, good-looking man. And you're expecting your third child," Zoey said, gently punching Darcy in the arm. "Between you and Beth we'll be spending a lot of time at the maternity floor of the hospital in a few months."

"That doesn't mean I can't look at a handsome man because that's as far as it goes. No one will take the place of Joshua in my heart."

Tanya listened to her friends talk about their husbands, their children, the babies Darcy and Beth were expecting. She was the only one not married in the group, and she felt the loneliness of her situation more now than ever. A few years ago—first with Crystal's riding accident, then Tom's arson conviction that led to him divorcing her and ultimately his death in prison—her whole life had fallen apart. She was still trying to put the pieces back together and keep her manic depression under control. And she would because she had no other choice. Crystal depended on her.

"Samuel said Chance wasn't sure how long he would stay in Sweetwater," Beth said, drawing Tanya back into the conversation.

She blinked, focusing on the group of women who had been there for her through all the tragedies. "Yeah, he said he wasn't sure how long he'll be here, especially if he doesn't get the job with Nick."

"So Nick's job brought him to Sweetwater?" Zoey took a sip of her iced tea.

"I think it was more than that. I think Samuel and his description of Sweetwater had a lot to do with it." Samuel was a great counselor, and Tanya wondered if that had something to do with Chance coming to town. She just couldn't shake the feeling he was hurting inside and needed help healing. She recognized the signs because she was in the same situation.

"Where's he from?" Darcy asked.

"Louisville."

"Well, it's perfect timing. You've got a tenant and some extra money when you needed it the most. Nick might have his assistant. God works in wondrous ways." Beth wiped her mouth and put the napkin beside her empty plate. "Samuel's certainly glad Chance decided to come, even if it's only for a while."

Jesse leaned close, covering Tanya's hand. "Just remember you're not alone. Nick and I can help you financially if you need it."

Overwhelmed by all their love, Tanya smiled,

fighting the lump rising in her throat. "I know. You've mentioned it half a dozen times. But as I said before, Jesse, I have to stand on my own two feet. No more handouts."

"Even with Samuel's stamp of approval, I think we should take this meeting over to Tanya's house and check this guy out." Zoey gathered up her purse as though she was preparing to leave.

"And scare him off? No way! If you all descend on him, he won't know what hit him. Remember, I need the extra money."

"Okay, we won't go over all at once. But I'll be there later this afternoon." Zoey rose.

Jesse slid from the large booth next. "I'll come over after church tomorrow."

"And I'll see you tomorrow evening," Beth added. "Samuel told me to tell you to bring Chance along to the barbecue."

Darcy, the last to exit the booth, lumbered to her feet, putting her hand at the small of her back. "That leaves Monday after you get off work. I'll come over after I visit my doctor." She patted her round stomach. "Twelve weeks to go, but then who's counting?"

"Certainly not you," Tanya said with a laugh. Standing in the midst of her circle of friends, she shook her head. "You all are gonna scare the man away, so I don't want any unexpected visits." She started for the café door. "You'll see him soon enough. Give him a chance to settle in."

Her friends' chuckles followed Tanya outside. She wouldn't put it past each one of them to ignore what she'd said and show up right on time. She was lucky to have friends like them.

Tanya slid into her six-year-old white van, equipped with a lift for Crystal's wheelchair, and backed out of her parking space. Turning down Third Avenue a few minutes later, she spied Chance, dressed in tan slacks and a black short-sleeved shirt, walking toward Berryhill Road with three large bags in his arms.

She pulled over to the curb and rolled down the window. "Want a ride?"

For a brief, few seconds he hesitated before he made his way toward the vehicle and placed one sack on the ground, then reached for the handle. After he climbed in, he settled two bags at his feet and one in his lap. "Thanks."

Did he get the job? Tanya wondered but didn't say anything. Instead, she drove in silence, aware of every minute movement Chance made. Even his clean, fresh scent saturated the air in the van.

Searching her mind for something to say, she

dug her teeth into her bottom lip, painfully aware of one of her shortcomings. She wasn't good at small talk, especially with strangers. Finally she lit upon a subject as she turned onto Berryhill Road. "It's been unusually warm for even the end of September. I love winter and cold weather, but I'm afraid if this keeps up we won't have much of one." Boy, you would think she could come up with a better topic than the weather!

Silence.

Okay, maybe she should try a question. "Which do you prefer?" She threw a glance toward Chance.

His brow creased. "Prefer?"

"Cold or hot weather?" Why couldn't she think of something better to talk about? Next, she would hear him snoring because she'd put him to sleep with her scintillating conversation.

"Cold."

"Oh, then we have something in common." The second she'd said the last sentence she'd wanted to take every word back. What she really wanted to talk about was the interview with Nick. But what if Chance hadn't gotten the job?

She slid another look toward him as she pulled into her driveway. The neutral expression on his face told her nothing of what he was thinking. She decided she couldn't wait for him to say anything about the interview. "Did Nick hire you?"

"Yes. I start Wednesday."

"That's great!" Why wasn't he more excited?

When she switched off the engine, Chance opened his door and hopped out. Before he had an opportunity to escape upstairs to his apartment, Tanya hurried around the front of the van and took the bag he'd set on the ground.

"I can come back for it," he said, striding toward the stairs.

She thought about her conversation with her friends at the café and the fact she wanted to get to know him better, not because she was interested in him as a man but because she needed to know more since he was her tenant. *Yeah, right, Tanya,* she silently scolded herself, knowing in her heart that wasn't the real reason.

"Nonsense. That's what neighbors are for— to help," she hurriedly said as he put half the length of the driveway between them.

She saw him flinch when she'd said neighbors and wondered about his reaction. Somebody had hurt him. A neighbor? When he shifted at the top of the stairs so he could unlock his door, she glimpsed that haunted look again that aroused her compassion and her curiosity.

Chance disappeared inside as Tanya put her foot on the first step. Quickening her pace, she half expected him to return to the landing and take the bag she carried, then bar her from entering his apartment. But when she reached the threshold, she found him across the room. He stood stiffly at the kitchen table, staring at the floor as though a memory had grabbed hold of him and wouldn't let go. The look that flashed across his face tore at her heart.

A board creaked as she moved inside. His head snapped up, his gaze snaring hers. A shutter descended over his expression, and he turned away and busied himself by emptying his bags.

"Are you all right?" she asked and crossed the large room. His expression earlier had for one brief moment reminded her of Tom's that first time she had gone to the prison to see him.

Chance stiffened, stopping for a few seconds before resuming his task. "I'm fine."

Although the words were spoken casually, she knew something she'd said had upset him. "I'm sorry if I—"

He pivoted toward her and took the sack from her. "Thanks for helping. I can take it from here."

In other words, get lost, Tanya thought but

wasn't ready to take the not-so-subtle hint. She didn't totally understand why, but she needed to help him, as though God was urging her to be there for him. Something in his past had caused him to stop believing. Her faith was the only thing that had held her life together over the past few years. Without Christ she would never have been able to piece the fragments together into a whole—albeit a fragile whole.

"That's okay. I don't mind helping. Crystal's at church at a youth group activity, and I don't have to pick her up for another twenty minutes." She began removing the groceries from the paper bag she'd brought in, ignoring the scowl on his face.

While she put the food on the table, Chance took the items and shelved them, each movement economical. The short sleeves of his black cotton shirt didn't hide the fact the man had well-defined muscles. This prodded the thought she should do something for exercise other than walking to and from the van.

He froze in midmotion. Her gaze lifted to his, and she saw a question in his eyes as he noted her interest. Heat scorched her cheeks. She didn't usually stare at anyone, least of all a man. And then to be caught doing it mortified her.

She averted her head and asked the first thing that popped into her mind, "Did you mean it when you said you'd help me with a budget?"

"I never say anything unless I mean it." He continued putting away his food, though thankfully his back was to her now.

If she'd had to look into his face, she would have fled the apartment. She couldn't believe she had openly stared at him again and then worse been caught doing it. She really had no experience when it came to men. The only one she had seriously dated had been Tom her senior year in high school. Not long after she'd graduated, they had married. Crystal had been born two years later.

"I could use your help," she murmured, surprised at her boldness in asking him for help.

"I can come over later tonight." He paused for several heartbeats. "Unless you have other plans."

Like a date, she thought, then nearly laughed out loud. There were some people in town who still thought she might have known about what Tom had been doing after Crystal's accident. If it weren't for her church and circle of friends, she would have left Sweetwater rather than endure their silent accusations that she had known Tom had been setting fire to all those barns. She'd never dreamed that her husband's rage at Crystal's accident and her paralysis would manifest itself that way. She'd been so wrapped up in dealing with Crystal's recovery and her own manic depression she hadn't seen the signs. Guilt still gnawed at her insides over not being there for Tom when he'd needed her the most. That guilt had plunged her into some dark times once, but she wouldn't allow it to again.

"I don't have any plans except picking Crystal up and then doing the chores that I leave for the weekend."

His gaze fixed on her. "I'll come over around eight then."

"That's fine." His loneliness, a palpable force, reached out to her and drew her to him.

She took a step toward Chance, grabbing a can of green beans and thrusting it at him. Her hand trembled as he took it, his fingers brushing against hers. Her breath caught in her throat as his look delved beneath her surface as if he searched for her innermost thoughts.

He opened his mouth to say something but instead snapped it close, spun around and placed the can on a shelf. "Great, then I'll see you later."

She was being dismissed again, but for some reason she didn't want to leave just yet. Even though tension vibrated in the air, a strong need to comfort—again she had no idea what or why—swamped her. She curled her hands into tight fists to keep from touching his arm.

"Listen, if there's anything—"

"Thanks, for helping me put my groceries up. If you're gonna pick up Crystal, you'd better get going." He turned his back to her and opened another cabinet door.

Tanya backed up several paces, saying, "You're right. I'd better leave." She whirled around and hurried from the apartment.

Out on the landing she paused and stared down at her driveway and the back of her house. She couldn't shake the feeling that God was pushing her toward Chance Taylor, that he needed a friend, someone to show him the power of the Lord. With quivering hands, she gripped the wooden railing.

Lord, how can I be Your instrument when my own life is so messed up?

No answer came to mind, leaving her feeling as though God was saying everyone can help another in need. *Is that true?* There was only one way to find out. She would be Chance's friend because she knew what it was like not to have one. She also knew the difference her friends had made in her life. No one should go through life without people to care about him, and for some reason, she sensed Chance was totally alone.

With a glance at her watch, she noted the time. She had to pick up Crystal in less than five minutes. Rushing down the stairs, she withdrew her keys from her jeans pocket then climbed into the van.

Ten minutes later she pulled into the parking lot next to the church and jogged toward the back door that led into the classrooms. Usually Crystal was waiting for her by the entrance, but today she wasn't around. As Tanya headed down the long hallway, she heard voices coming from the last room on the left where the youth group met.

She started to enter when her daughter's words halted her.

"I don't know what to do about them, Sean."

"Ignore them. They aren't worth your time."

"I wish I could."

The sob in Crystal's voice contracted Tanya's heart. She hurried inside. "Honey, are you all right?"

With her daughter's back to her, she couldn't see Crystal's face as she answered, "Yeah, sure."

"I'm sorry I'm late." Tanya took a step forward.

"You aren't that late. Sean's been keeping me company."

A strange expression flitted across Darcy's son's features before he pulled himself together. "Yeah, Mrs. Bolton. Crystal's been receiving a lot of spam lately on the Internet."

If Tanya hadn't sensed the seriousness of the situation, she would have choked on her laughter. "Spam?"

Crystal finally swung her wheelchair around. "Yeah, I went to the wrong web site by mistake and now I'm getting all kinds of spam."

Tanya knew that probably wasn't what Sean and Crystal had been talking about, but she also knew by the tilt to her daughter's chin she wouldn't get it out of her until Crystal was ready to tell her. Her daughter had been keeping a lot of secrets lately. But that didn't mean Tanya wouldn't do some more checking around. When she had talked with Zoey and Beth earlier about this, they hadn't known what was going on but said they would look into it for her. "I guess I can take a look at it, but I don't know much about computers."

Sean shot to his feet. "That's okay. I'll come over tomorrow after church and see what I can do."

"That's great. See, Crystal, how easy the problem can be fixed? From what Darcy says, Sean can do anything with a computer."

"Yeah, Mom," her daughter mumbled with her head down, her hands twisting together in her lap. "This may not be that easy to take care of."

The sound of his feet pounding against the pavement lured him into a rhythmic trance as Chance ran down Berryhill Road, heading toward his temporary home. Sweat drenched his white T-shirt and face. He almost went past the one-story older house with a detached garage and apartment above it. He jogged a few yards beyond, slowed and circled back around.

Freedom, as he hadn't experienced in years, called to him. He wanted to keep going, but his body screamed with exhaustion, not used to this form of exercise—not for the two years he'd spent incarcerated.

He came to a stop at the end of the driveway and bent over, drawing in lungfuls of rich oxygen, the air scented with the smells of the clean outdoors, nothing stale and musty about it. The rich colors that surrounded him no longer threw him.

He had dreamed for so long about running with the wind cooling his skin and the sun beating down to warm his chilled body that he could hardly believe he was finally doing it. He'd taken so much for granted before—not any more, not ever again. He cherished each fresh breath of freedom, each precious day he could walk out of a place unhindered, each time he could close his eyes and not worry about whether he would wake up the next morning or not. His life began the day he'd walked out of prison.

Was his new job thrusting him back into a world he didn't want to be in? He needed a job and had been glad for a reference from Samuel, but the more he thought about the duties Nick wanted his assistant to do the more he felt as though he was being thrust back into the corporate life he'd wanted to avoid, that very life that had required hours and hours of overtime. If he had been with his wife and daughter when they had come home to find a stranger in their house, then maybe they would be alive today.

Still he needed the job. He would just have to take it one day at a time and not let his job consume his whole life. Not ever again.

With his heartbeat slowing, he strode toward the stairs that led to his apartment. A quick look toward the left halted his progress. Crystal sat on the deck, drawing something on a pad. Suddenly she threw down her pencil, tore off the sheet and crunched it into a ball. She tossed it into the yard where several other similar papers lay crumpled.

The frustration and anger that marked the

teenager's face drew him toward her. If his daughter were alive, he would want to be there for her. That was impossible, of course, but he could help Tom's daughter.

"Nothing working out?" Chance gestured toward the wadded-up papers in the grass.

Crystal took the pencil her service dog had retrieved for her and looked up at him. "What's the use? I'm not any good anyway."

He descended the two steps to the yard and smoothed out one of the sheets. He whistled. "If this isn't good, then I hate to think what you consider bad. Who is this?" He came back to sit in the lounge chair next to her.

"Just a guy. No one important."

"Are all those attempts of him?"

Crystal nodded, peering away.

"Do you always waste your time drawing someone who isn't important to you?"

She sighed, then shook her head. "He doesn't know I'm alive."

The anguish that wrenched her voice did the same to him. He cleared his throat and asked, "How do you know?"

"I just do. I might as well be dead for all he cares."

The pain her words produced stole his breath. "I'm sorry. I…" Words failed him.

Chapter Three

For a brief moment Chance thought of his daughter. He remembered Haley making a comment a few days before she'd been killed about how she would just die if she didn't get to go to a friend's party. Haley never made it to the birthday party. He turned away, aware that Crystal had clasped his arm while her service dog licked his hand.

"Are you okay, Chance?"

The alarm in her voice swung his gaze to Crystal. He forced a grin that was an effort to maintain. "I'm fine. I had a daughter. She would have been near your age if she'd lived." He couldn't believe he'd said that out loud. He didn't talk about Haley—he couldn't without—

"Oh, I'm so sorry. What happened?"

Gone were Crystal's problems as she leaned

toward him, wanting to offer comfort. Most of the time he could handle it. Coming to Sweet-water had for some reason revived all those memories. Probably because Crystal was so close in age to Haley. There was only a year between them.

"She was killed." He scooted forward in the chair. "But I don't want to talk about me. Tell me about this guy you have a crush on."

Crystal started to say something but decided not to. Instead, she shrugged. "There's nothing to say. He's popular. I'm not." She put her hand on her service dog, stroking her Lab's black fur. "He's on the basketball team. Even though he's a freshman, he plays varsity because he's so good. The season will start in six weeks. I try to go to every game."

"You like basketball," he said, sensing Crystal steering the conversation away from the guy she cared about.

Her face lit. "Yes. I've even tried to play some with Sean. He's my best friend."

"Are you any good?"

Laughter invaded her features. "Are you kidding? I can't even hit the backboard now. I use to be able to before the accident. But I can still dribble."

"Maybe all you need is practice. I could fix

you up a basketball hoop and backboard if you want."

"Really?"

He nodded, her enthusiasm contagious. "If it's okay with your mom."

"What's okay with me?"

The screen door banged closed, and Tanya strolled toward him. Her smile of greeting, reaching deep into her eyes, soothed some of the tension knotting his stomach. He came to his feet, facing Tanya, who was only a few inches shorter than his own six foot plus height.

"I offered to put up a basketball hoop for Crystal."

Her mahogany eyes grew dull. She ran her hand through her short brown hair, brushing back her wispy bangs. "I don't want—I appreciate the offer, but I'm sure you have better things to do."

He grinned, wanting to tease the smile back into her eyes, needing to lighten the mood. "Nope. I don't have anything to do except shop for some new clothes between now and Wednesday. So I'm pretty much a man of leisure in need of a project."

"Mom?"

Tanya glanced at her daughter. Eagerness replaced her earlier sadness. For the past three years Tanya had constantly depended on others to make it through. Each day she felt herself growing stronger. And with that, she had determined she would learn to stand on her own two feet. She didn't want to become any more beholden to Chance Taylor than she was. She'd already regretted asking him to help her with her budget. But how could she turn her daughter down? Basketball and drawing were the two things Crystal loved the most.

"Fine. But only if you let me help you. And I'm paying for the materials." Somehow she would come up with the money for the hoop, backboard and wood to secure it to the garage.

"Good. See you two later."

Tanya watched Chance stroll away, his hair damp from exercise, a fine sheen of sweat covering his face. He must have gone for a long run. He'd been gone over an hour. She should do more exercise. *I wonder if he would like a running partner,* she thought, realizing she'd probably never go jogging unless she did it with someone.

"Thanks, Mom."

Crystal's voice dragged her from her musings. "You're welcome. Next time, honey, say something to me first. I could have figured out how to put one up."

Her daughter giggled. "This from the woman

who until recently didn't know what a Phillips head screwdriver was?"

"But I do now. I'm getting quite handy around the house, if I do say so myself."

"I didn't ask him, Mom. He volunteered when we were talking about basketball. Did you know he had a daughter? She died."

"Really! That's horrible." Tanya peered toward the apartment over her garage, beginning to see why there was such a look of vulnerability about Chance Taylor. Losing a child was the worst thing she could imagine. She remembered when Crystal had first been taken to the hospital almost four years ago. The feeling of devastation had thrown her life into a tailspin that slowly she had managed to right, but not without a lot of heartache along the way.

"Do you think that's why he wants to help me out?"

"Possibly, honey." Then Tanya grinned. "But more likely because you're such a sweet child."

Crystal screwed up her face into a pout. "I'm not a child anymore, Mom, in case you haven't noticed."

Her daughter's fervent words wiped the smile from Tanya's face. "Oh, ba—Crystal, I've noticed what a beautiful young lady you're growing up to be."

"Then you're the only one," Crystal mumbled and wheeled herself into the house.

Stunned at the despondency in her daughter's voice, Tanya quickly followed Crystal inside only to find the door to her room closed with her Do Not Disturb sign hanging from the knob. She knocked.

"Go away."

"Crystal, we need to talk."

"I don't have anything else to say," her daughter said right before the sound of loud music blasted through the air.

Tanya stared at the door, trying to decide whether to ignore her child's request or wait for another time when she would be more willing to talk. *Lord, help me here. What do I do?*

The music grew even louder, silently giving Tanya her answer. Nothing would be accomplished this evening finding out what was at the root of her daughter's unhappiness.

"I noticed you've owned this house for ten years. Why don't you take out a second mortgage on it?" Chance asked Tanya later that evening.

"Well…" She didn't have an answer for him. Sitting at her kitchen table with all her finances spread out before her, she stared at the total figure of her debt, in large black numbers on the paper before her. "I didn't want another bill to pay."

"You could use it to pay off some of these bills and consolidate them into one payment. That'll be easier for you to keep track of rather than these seven different places." He waved his hand over the pile.

"That might work."

Chance wrote down some numbers. "I think you could comfortably handle this much a month in a payment."

"Only as long as I have a tenant for the apartment."

He looked up from the paper he was figuring on. "Since I've taken a job with Blackburn Industries, I'll be here for a while."

Why had that simple declaration sent her heart racing as though she had just finished running alongside him earlier this afternoon? "It's gonna be more than a while until I can pay this off."

"You can always declare bankruptcy."

"No! Never! I'll pay my debts even if it takes me years." The memory of her father skipping out on her mother and her when she was a little girl materialized in her mind. The gambling debts he'd left behind had been overwhelming until her mother had nearly collapsed under their weight. But it had been a matter of pride to her mother that she didn't declare bankruptcy, sometimes the only thing that had kept her going.

"Then a second mortgage is the best way to go. I've written down a budget that should help you stay on track." He slid the paper across the table to her.

She picked it up and studied it. One large, long-term debt versus many smaller ones. She liked the idea. "I can check into it at the bank on Monday. This way I can finish paying the law—" She pressed her lips shut, wanting to snatch her last sentence back. She slanted a look at Chance to see his reaction.

He calmly stacked the sheets into a nice pile as though she hadn't spoken. "Legal fees can be staggering."

When she didn't get the question about what kind of legal fees, she relaxed back in the chair, inhaling several, calming breaths. "I can also pay a lot of the hospital bill, too. Of course, it'll depend on how much I can get as a second mortgage. I wish I was better with money." She leaned toward him and got a whiff of the soap he must have used when taking a shower. She thought of a green hillside in the spring and for a second forgot what she was going to say.

His gaze connected with hers. The beating of her heart echoed in her ears as she became lost in the sky blue of his eyes.

One corner of his mouth quirked up. "How long have you been a teller?"

"Almost two years. Don't tell the bank manager what I said about handling money. It can be our little secret."

"My lips are sealed."

A twinkle danced in his eyes, and she lowered her regard to those lips he mentioned. All she could focus on was the way they curved slightly at the end in that smile she had decided was lethal.

She slid her gaze away and took the stack of papers, then stuffed them into the manila envelopes she kept them in. Her hands shook, and she nearly dropped all of them. She scooted her chair back. The scraping sound across the tile echoed through the kitchen. After she rose, she walked to the desk by the phone and crammed them in the top drawer.

"There. Out of sight, out of mind, at least for the rest of the evening."

"Money worries can be very hard on a person."

"You speak as though you've had firsthand knowledge." She lounged back on the desk with her hands digging into the wooden edge and braced herself for him to either ignore her or shut the topic down.

He stared out the window that afforded him a view of Crystal on the deck with her service dog. "I've helped many clients in the past come up with a plan to get out of debt. Some make it. Others don't."

There was more to it than that, but his evasive look alerted her to the fact she wouldn't get an answer from him until he was ready. Had he been like one of those clients, in debt, struggling to make ends meet? For some reason she didn't think that was it, even though he had few possessions that she knew of and he had arrived in town on a bus.

Tanya pushed herself away from the desk. "I intend to be one of your success stories."

"Good." He stood. "I'd better go. It's getting late." His glance strayed again to the window that overlooked the deck. "Is something wrong with Crystal? She hardly said two words tonight."

"You know how moody teenage girls can be. She's upset with me and even ate her dinner in her room before going outside on the deck."

"Yes, I know what..." His voice trailed off into the silence.

"Oh, I'm sorry. I shouldn't have said anything. Crystal told me you had a daughter who died."

He closed his eyes for a few seconds, then when he opened them again, there was a raw look in their blue depths that turned them the color of the lake right before a storm. "I lost both my wife and daughter a few years back."

"I'm so sorry. My husband died last spring, so I understand what you must have gone through."

An expression full of doubt flickered across his face for a few seconds before he managed to mask it. He walked to the back door and thrust it open, then disappeared quickly. Tanya heard him say something to her daughter. She observed the exchange, saw Crystal's features coming alive while she spoke to Chance. She even laughed, which thrilled Tanya. Her daughter hadn't laughed much lately—ever since the start of high school six weeks before.

Chance sensed Tanya's gaze on him and shifted his weight from one foot to the other. In prison he'd gotten used to being watched all the time, but that didn't mean he liked the feeling. It made him think of a bug under a microscope, every movement noted and analyzed.

"May I pet your dog?" he asked Crystal, the hairs on his nape prickling.

"Sure. Charlie loves people."

"He's a beauty." Chance stroked the length

of the black Lab's back. "So what are you writing about?"

"About the prejudice in the book *To Kill a Mockingbird.*"

"How far have you gotten?"

"I'm almost finished with the rough draft. We're supposed to compare and contrast it to the prejudice in our society today."

"How's that coming?" Chance asked, having experienced his own kind of prejudice when he had been released from prison three weeks ago. Although his conviction had been overturned, people still looked at him strangely, and he could see the question of his innocence lurking in their gazes.

"The comparing and contrasting has been the easiest part. You know, not all prejudice is racial."

"True. People can be prejudiced against anyone, an overweight person or someone who stutters. There's all kinds."

"I know."

Chance studied Crystal's solemn expression, illuminated in the light by the door. "Is something going on at school?"

Her gaze slid away from his, her head dropping until her chin nearly touched her chest.

"Crystal? What's happening?"

"Nothing," she mumbled.

He knelt and leaned close because he'd barely heard her reply. "Is someone bothering you?"

She didn't say anything.

"Crystal?" Something was wrong. Tension oscillated in waves from the teenager.

"It's really nothing. I can handle it."

He bent down farther until he caught her gaze and held it. "You'll tell someone if you can't?"

She lifted her head, visibly swallowed and nodded. She shivered. "It's getting cold. I'd better go in. Night." She guided her wheelchair toward the back door and waited for Charlie to open it for her.

Chance didn't leave the deck until the teenager had disappeared inside. Through the open blinds he saw Tanya say something to her daughter, following Crystal out of the room. He'd speak to Tanya tomorrow about what her daughter had implied. If someone was harassing Crystal, it needed to stop, especially with her earlier comment about the guy she was attempting to draw. Was he the one bothering her?

Chance hurried up the stairs two at a time and entered his apartment. Tom had been there for him in prison. He would be there for Tom's daughter. He owed the man his life.

Having no books, radio or television, he decided to go to bed early. He intended to start the basketball hoop for Crystal early the next morning if he could find a store open on Sunday that sold lumber and the other supplies he would need. He wanted to give the teenager something to smile about.

In the dark he stretched out on the double bed with his arms folded behind his head. Staring up at the ceiling, he reviewed the day's activities. He had a job. Only time would tell whether it was the best one for him. He'd assisted Tanya with her budget and he knew now how to help Crystal. Not too bad.

"I'll protect them, Tom," he whispered into the blackness, his eyelids growing heavy with sleep....

Three men with exaggerated grins and taunting voices surrounded him. Chance glanced from one to the other. When his gaze finally settled on the ringleader, tall and thin but with arms like steel clubs, Chance's heart thudded against his chest. The instigator of this little impromptu meeting clenched his fist around a homemade knife, the blade long—three, exaggerated feet—and sharp. His cackles chilled the air in the cell as though a blizzard had swept through the prison, freezing everything but them.

Trapped, with his back against the bars, Chance didn't have to look around to know he wouldn't be able to walk away from them without a fight. He prepared himself, bracing his feet apart, balling his hands.

The ringleader charged, letting out a blood-curdling scream that plunged the temperature in the cell even colder. Suddenly from out of nowhere, Tom flew between him and the tall, thin man, planting himself in front of the long, long knife. The inmate brought the weapon back and shoved it toward Tom and him. The blade went through Tom's chest to skewer Chance.

Chance bolted up in bed, rivers of sweat running off him as he tried to draw in a decent breath. His lungs hurt as though he really had been pierced by a knife. He couldn't seem to inhale enough air. The pounding of his heart thundered in his ears, the nightmare relived yet again. When would it ever go away? Would Tom's death haunt him forever? He dug his fingers into the bedding, trying to focus on the pain emanating from them rather than his heart.

He knew one thing. He had to tell Tanya where he'd been for the past few years. He didn't want her to find out from someone else. He owed her that much.

* * *

Tanya pulled into her driveway after church, stopped at the side of her house and stared at the scene before her. Shock trembled through her. Chance was painting a basketball backboard bright yellow. The color glittered in the bright sunlight.

"I didn't think he would do it today," Tanya murmured, amazed at how fast Chance had managed to put the hoop up. She and Crystal had only been gone three hours.

"Do what, Mom?" Crystal asked from the back of the van where her wheelchair was locked into place.

"Chance has already put up that basketball hoop for you."

"He has?" Her daughter's own astonishment sounded in her voice. "I want to see."

Tanya slipped from the front and went to the back of the van to let down Crystal in her wheelchair. Charlie bounded out before her daughter. The second she was on the ground Crystal spun about and drove toward Chance who climbed down the ladder as she approached.

A grin, wide and contagious, graced his mouth. "Well, what do you think?" He pointed toward the finished product.

Tanya noticed a streak of yellow paint

slashing across his cheek. She clasped her hands together to still the urge to wipe it off. Much too intimate a gesture for someone she'd only met a few days before. Yet it seemed so natural for her to do it.

"I made it so you could adjust the height of the hoop some. Right now it's a little lower than normal. Once you master this height, I can raise it."

His comment to Crystal made it seem as though he intended to stay in Sweetwater, at least for the time being. Even though she knew he had the job with Nick, the realization Chance would be around sent a current of warmth through Tanya that she hadn't experienced in years.

Her daughter beamed as though the sun shone in her smile. "I'm gonna get my basketball." With Charlie beside her, Crystal steered her wheelchair toward the ramp that led to the deck.

"Thank you, Chance. She hasn't smiled much lately."

"Do you know anything about a boy she has a crush on at school?"

The question stunned Tanya. She knew her daughter was growing up, but Crystal hadn't said anything to her, and they had always had a close relationship, especially because of all they had been through together the past four years. "No, who?"

"I don't know. But the other day she used up a lot of paper trying to draw him. She was never satisfied. When I said something to her about him, she said he didn't know she was alive."

Her breath jammed in her throat. Was this what had been bothering Crystal? She had a crush on someone who didn't return the feelings? Tanya's heart squeezed, an intense pressure building in her chest. How could she protect Crystal from being hurt?

"She hasn't said anything to me. I'll do some checking and see what I can find out. Something has been wrong with her lately so it's possible this might be it." Although she doubted that was what had made her daughter so unhappy lately, she would investigate. Remembering the day before and the conversation she'd interrupted between Crystal and Sean, Tanya couldn't shake the feeling her daughter was being harassed.

Chance studied her for a few seconds. "But you don't think it is?"

"No." She started to tell him what she thought it might really be, when she heard the back door closing and glanced toward her daughter making her way toward them. "Don't say anything to Crystal about us talking about the boy. It would only upset her."

"Sure, but if I can help, let me know."

Tanya tilted her head to the side and studied Chance. "Why do you want to help? Up until a few days ago we were strangers."

"Samuel told me about how rough it has been the past few years for you."

She pulled up straight, her arms rigid at her sides. "I won't take anyone's charity. Crystal and I can get along just fine by ourselves." She whirled around and started for the back door when a hand clamped around her arm.

Chapter Four

❧

"I just want to help, Tanya." Chance released his grasp almost immediately after touching her.

But Tanya felt the imprint of his fingers on her upper arm as though he branded her. She glanced at where they had lain for a few electrified seconds, then up into his eyes, full of regret. "I can't take pity, Chance. I've had my fill of that in my life."

"No pity. Your daughter—" he peered at Crystal making her way toward them and pitched his voice low as he continued "—she reminds me of my daughter. It helps to help her—and you."

All anger dissolved as Tanya turned completely toward him, wanting to comfort, wishing she had the right to embrace him, to let him know he wasn't alone. But she didn't want him to think she pitied him because she knew, like her, he wouldn't appreciate that. "I want to pay for the supplies. That's the least I can do since you did all the work."

The sound of a basketball striking against the concrete of the driveway drew closer. Tanya looked toward her daughter and managed to give her a smile. "Sean said something about coming over this afternoon. Maybe you two could practice some."

"I gave him a call. His mom is bringing him now." Crystal continued to dribble.

"Give it a try," Chance said to her daughter who kept looking at the backboard.

"I think I'll wait till Sean gets here. Thanks, Chance." Crystal flashed him a smile, the basketball connecting with the driveway a rhythmic sound in the sudden quiet. "Mom made some lemonade. Want some?"

Chance chuckled, swiping the back of his hand across his forehead. "That sounds great." He swung his full attention to Tanya and whispered, "I think your daughter wants us to get lost so she can practice."

"But who will get the ball for her?"

"She'll manage. Besides, she has Charlie. I wouldn't be surprised if she teaches him to retrieve it for her."

Tanya began walking toward the back door. "I do have some lemonade that you are welcome to have."

Chance dropped his gaze to his cutoff jeans and dirty, sweaty T-shirt. "Although it does sound great, I think I'd better pass on it. I need a shower."

"Oh, I almost forgot. Beth and Samuel want us to bring you to a barbecue they're having this evening at their house."

"What time?"

"Six. Casual attire."

His grin dimpled his cheeks. "Good, because that's all I have at the moment."

Chance headed for his apartment and that shower. At the entrance, he stopped and glanced back at Crystal. A young man jogged up the driveway. Chance waited before entering. When Tanya's daughter smiled a greeting, he decided the teenager must be Sean and went inside.

He should have taken Tanya up on that glass of lemonade and used the time away from Crystal to explain about being in prison with Tom. The words had been on the tip of his tongue for a few seconds, then Crystal had returned with her ball and the moment passed. There was a part of him that realized he was making excuses which wasn't like him. But so many changes had occurred over the past few years. He hated to think being a coward was one of them.

No! He would tell her tonight after the barbecue. No matter what.

"You know the others are going be jealous that I'm the first to see your mysterious tenant." Beth took a huge salad bowl out of the refrigerator in her kitchen.

"So that's what was behind Chance's invitation tonight," Tanya said with a laugh.

"Well, not exactly, just a plus. Samuel wants Chance to feel at home here in Sweetwater." Beth stepped closer and looked around as though to make sure no one else was in the room and added, "I think he hopes Chance will settle down here permanently. If that happens, that will certainly solve a problem for you."

The heat of a blush singed Tanya's cheeks. "What problem?" That she was dateless and gun-shy? she wondered but kept that to herself.

"Why, your apartment needing a tenant. What did you think I meant?" Beth pinned her with an amused look.

Tanya refused to squirm under her friend's scrutiny. "Sometimes I think all of you have taken after Jesse and her matchmaking ways. Remember trying to fix me up with Darrell?"

"Oh, that." Beth waved her hand. "I just wanted to help a fellow teacher feel at home since he moved to Sweetwater two months ago."

Tanya harrumphed, knowing good and well that wasn't all there was to it. Since she had become the only unmarried member of her circle of friends, she had noticed an increased interest in making sure she met every unmarried male Jesse, Darcy, Beth and Zoey knew, which made for quite a few.

"How's the morning sickness been?" Tanya asked, deciding to take the focus off her and dating—or rather, lack of dating.

"Much better. I haven't had any trouble in a week. And now that I've started wearing maternity clothes, my outfits are more comfortable."

"The next four or five months will go by so fast. Before you know it, your baby will be here. And then the work will really start."

Beth pulled a set of salad tongs out of the drawer. "I understand Sean helped Crystal today shoot baskets."

"Is there a secret left in this town? That just happened this afternoon."

"I didn't know Crystal shooting baskets was supposed to be a secret. The basketball hoop is out in the open where anyone can see it. It's a bright yellow. A little hard *not* to see it, if you ask me."

Peering out the window, Tanya found her daughter sitting with Craig, Beth's stepson, talking. "I don't think she wants it known all over town. I think someone is harassing Crystal at school. I wouldn't want the fact she's practicing basketball to be something she'll get teased about. She loves the game and that could kill it."

"Harassing Crystal? Who?"

"She won't say. She has a crush on a boy who doesn't return the feelings. It could be him, but I don't think so."

"Let me do some checking around, discreetly, of course. If someone is, I'll find out and let you know. That's unacceptable behavior at Sweetwater High."

"It's unacceptable behavior anywhere, but you and I know it goes on all the time."

"Sadly, it's true. C'mon. Let's join the men." Beth grabbed not only the large salad bowl but two bottles of dressing.

"What can I take outside?"

"I have tea already on the table, but get the pitcher of ice water just in case someone wants that instead."

Tanya withdrew the green plastic pitcher from the refrigerator and started for the door.

Beth paused before opening it and peered over her shoulder at Tanya. "I also heard that Chance built the basketball hoop for Crystal. That was nice of him. He's very helpful to have around."

Tanya narrowed her eyes on her good friend. "And?"

"Nothing. Just an observation I was making."

"And half the townspeople, I bet."

"What can I say?" Beth shrugged, then pulled the door open.

Chance, being the closest person to Beth and Tanya, relieved Beth of the bottles of dressing and placed them on the long picnic table, already set for dinner. Her friend murmured her thanks, her gaze shifting to Tanya as though she shared a secret with Tanya. She glanced away, feeling the warmth creep up her face. Honestly, some people in town were downright nosy. She'd forgotten that about Sweetwater. She shouldn't have since not that long ago she had been the major object of gossip with her husband's arson conviction, his demand for a divorce and then his death last spring. And from that, she knew she didn't like being the center of attention one bit. Thankfully the past few months everything had settled down.

"Come and get it," Samuel called out to the

kids as he placed the grilled meat on the red tablecloth.

Allie, Craig and Jane, Samuel's three children from his previous marriage, hurried toward the picnic table. Crystal followed in her wheelchair and positioned it at one end while Tanya sat on her daughter's left and Chance on the right. For just a brief moment it seemed as though they were two families sitting down to enjoy a meal together. Then Tanya had to remind herself that wasn't exactly right—even when Chance's gaze captured hers and held it for a few extra seconds while the Morgans sat down.

"Let's pray," Samuel said and bowed his head over his empty plate.

After saying his thanks to the Lord, Samuel began passing the food—a platter of barbecue chicken, the tossed green salad and a bowl of corn on the cob, cooked over the grill. The various aromas of the meal wafted to Tanya, teasing her appetite and making her stomach rumble.

"Well, at least I know that Tanya is hungry," Beth said, laughter dancing in her eyes.

"I forgot to eat lunch. I'm not hungry. I'm *starved*." Tanya took the platter and forked a piece of chicken, then passed the food to her daughter.

When everyone's plate was full, Samuel

asked Chance, "What do you think of Sweetwater so far?"

"That's a loaded question."

"First impressions."

"Welcoming, friendly and beautiful with the lake nearby. When I went jogging yesterday and today, I had several people stop me to introduce themselves. When they heard we were friends, I got the rundown on you and the fine job you're doing as the Reverend of Sweetwater Community Church." Chance stopped for a few seconds, moving his food around on his plate before he added, "Several today wanted to know why I wasn't in church this morning."

Knowing the subject was a touchy one for Chance, Tanya said, "I keep promising myself that I'll start jogging, but I never seem to get around to doing it."

"What's stopping you?" Chance asked, his gaze linking with hers.

For a few seconds a connection zapped between them, making Tanya wish that they were alone so she could pursue his reluctance to attend church. Somehow she felt it was at the heart of what had wounded him. "I'm not very motivated to exercise since it isn't one of my favorite things to do. I know it would be a good thing to do, but it's so much easier to come up with a reason not to jog. It's not hard to talk myself out of it when I think about it. There's always laundry to do or the house to clean."

"You need a jogging partner," Beth said and pointedly looked from Tanya to Chance.

Tanya took a sip of her tea to hide her smile at the obvious hint her friend had thrown out to Chance.

Being the gentleman she was discovering Chance was, he asked, "Want to jog with me tomorrow?"

"Tomorrow I work late. I won't be home until after six. I usually grab something for Crystal and me to eat on the way home."

"That's okay. I can wait until then."

"I doubt I could keep up with you."

Chance chuckled. "You *are* good at coming up with excuses. I haven't been running for long. Don't worry about me. I'll stop by at seven, and we can go jogging by the lake until it gets dark or one of us tires."

"Well, then it's settled, Tanya. You've got yourself a jogging partner." Beth shifted her attention to Crystal. "How's the paper coming?"

"Done."

"Good. I've enjoyed reading your work. You're a talented writer, Crystal."

"This paper was easy."

"You wouldn't know it from the moans from some of your classmates. There are so many ways you can deal with the subject of prejudice in our society. You would think I asked them to write a book instead of five hundred words."

"That's a good subject for a sermon." Samuel lifted a chicken leg and took a bite.

As each Morgan gave his or her opinion about prejudice, Tanya slid a glance toward her daughter who was suddenly quiet, her head down as she played with her food, eating little. She also noticed Chance didn't say much, either.

As Jane declared, "You can't let people get away with putting you down. You've got to stand up to them." Tanya saw Crystal stiffen. Her reaction to the conversation only confirmed Tanya's earlier suspicion.

"Goodness, Tanya and Crystal probably aren't used to the lively discussions we have at the dinner table." Samuel caught Tanya's attention. "Sorry, we got carried away. Let's solve the world's problems another night. We've got guests." His gaze swept each person sitting at the table to make sure his point was understood.

Silence ruled for a few minutes while everyone finished eating.

When Beth went inside to get the dessert,

Samuel said, "Chance, if you've got any free time with your new job, I sure could use someone to help with the finances at the new youth center. Think you have some time?"

"Sure." He would help Samuel any way he could since the reverend had been there for him on more than one occasion.

"You might even want to help out at the center," Samuel added with a grin as his wife came out with a chocolate cake.

While Beth sliced the dessert and passed the pieces around, Chance pictured himself entrenched in the life of Sweetwater. He rubbed his sweaty palm over the napkin in his lap before reaching for his fork to eat his cake. A job. Working at the youth center. Next, he would start going to Samuel's church. He knew that would make Samuel and Tanya happy, but he couldn't go under false pretenses. That wasn't right.

"I have some cake left. Anyone want seconds?" Beth asked with Samuel and Craig sliding their plates toward her.

Twenty minutes later after Tanya had helped clear the table and he and Samuel had made sure the backyard was cleaned up, Tanya announced, "We probably better go. Tomorrow's a school day."

"Don't remind me. I still have some papers to grade." Beth hugged Tanya and Crystal. "See you in class."

On the too-short drive back to Tanya's house, Chance tried to decide how best to bring up the subject of him being in prison. *Tanya, I knew your ex-husband because I was in the same cell block.* No, that wasn't good. *Tanya, I was innocent, but I went to prison for murder.*

No! I can't say that. But what can I say?

No answer came to mind as Tanya pulled into her driveway and climbed out to man the lift for Crystal. Charlie and the teenager headed for the ramp while Tanya grabbed her purse from the front seat. Crystal let herself into the house.

A light beaming down from the garage near the basketball hoop pooled around Chance. He stuffed his hands into his pockets and tried to form the words to explain his past. Tanya turned toward him, her mouth opening to say something. It snapped closed, her forehead knitting.

"What's wrong?" she asked, moving toward him.

Tell her. He sucked in a deep breath to alleviate the tightness in his chest. It didn't work. He felt as though he were suffocating. Again he drew in some oxygen-rich air and slowly the band about his torso loosened.

"Chance?"

"I need to talk to you. Do you have a minute?"

She peered toward the kitchen door then back at him. "Yes." She came even closer until she shared the pool of light with him.

Another deep breath flooded his senses with her scent of lilacs. He thought of a garden in the springtime with Tanya standing in the middle, sun warming her, birds singing, butterflies flittering from flower to flower. The picture brought him peace, and the constriction about him fell away.

"Up until three weeks ago I was in the state penitentiary...." He paused for a heartbeat. "For murder. My conviction was overturned because the real killer was found and is awaiting trial in Louisville."

As he made his rushed announcement, the color drained from Tanya's features, her body going stiff, her eyes growing round. Silence hung between them for a long moment. Chance saw a myriad of emotions flash across her face—shock, followed by anger, then finally a wary acceptance with a touch of pain in her eyes.

She brought her hand up to smooth back her wispy bangs. Her fingers trembled. "Did you know Tom?" she asked in a voice that quavered.

He nodded, his throat closed. He hadn't wanted to hurt her, to bring up bad memories, but he saw them in her eyes. Raw pain dominated her features now.

"Is that where you met Samuel?"

He pushed down his own reeling emotions, determined to finish this conversation with Tanya. "Yes. I became friends with Samuel—and Tom."

"Why did you come to Sweetwater?"

Tell her all of it. The words wouldn't come. He couldn't hurt her anymore. And worse, he didn't want to be sent away—at least, not until he had fulfilled his promise to himself, so he settled on part of the truth. "Samuel and Tom both told me about the town and it seemed like a good place to start over, to put my life back together."

"Who were you accused of murdering?" Again she lifted her hand and combed her quivering fingers through her short hair.

He'd known that question would be eventually asked, but hearing it created a deep ache in his heart that spread to encompass his whole body. "My wife and daughter," he whispered in a voice roughened with the memories. He had found them, and he would never forget the picture of them, lifeless, staring up at him but not seeing him.

"Oh, Chance." Tanya's face crumpled, tears

glistening in her eyes. "That's how you lost your family, to a killer?" she asked in a raspy voice.

The worst part was seeing the effect his words had on Tanya. When a tear escaped, he couldn't resist brushing his finger across her cheek, the feel of her warm skin riveting him to the present. "Yes, they surprised an intruder when they returned unexpectedly."

"Then why did *you* go to prison?"

Her innocent question produced a humorless laugh that died almost immediately. "That wasn't what the police originally thought, because my neighbor had overheard a very loud argument between Ruth and me a few hours before. I had to go in to work again and she wasn't happy with all the hours I was spending at the office. We had been fighting a lot about that subject. Some of our arguments were loud."

"Married couples fight. That's normal."

Chance looked off into the darkness that surrounded them. "My fingerprints were on the gun found at the scene because it was mine. The intruder had used my own gun to kill my family. There wasn't any sign of a break-in. So I became the prime suspect, and they stopped looking for an intruder even though there were a few pieces of expensive jewelry missing. The police felt that I had done that to cover up that I had killed them." Even to this day, it was almost inconceivable that the authorities had ever thought he would murder his own child.

Tanya moved to the stairs that led to his apartment and collapsed on the second step. She turned her face up toward him, but he couldn't see her expression in the dark. "How did they find the real killer?"

"This past year there were a series of robberies where the man snuck into garages when the homeowners were leaving. While they were gone, he would rob them and leave without anyone knowing until they couldn't find their jewelry or whatever he stole. Usually he took small, easily fenced items. He would case the houses, so he knew when the occupants would most likely leave and hide near the garage until they did. Then he would slip inside. A lot of people don't lock the door from the garage into their house. He would count on that."

"Until he did something wrong?" He didn't have to see her to know that anger laced her voice. But was it directed at him or the intruder?

Chance leaned against the railing, his hands gripping the wood so tight he felt a splinter dig into his palm. He didn't want to relive this, but he owed Tanya that much. "Yeah, the thief invaded a home that wasn't totally empty. The homeowner was a former Marine and knew how to take care of himself. When they searched the thief's place, the police found all the jewelry missing from my house. He had kept it because it was too hot to get rid of right after—after the murders." The words clogged his throat. He swallowed and continued in a husky voice, "I think he forgot about the jewelry. He lived with his mother. He hadn't robbed anyone for eighteen months because he had been in jail for assault. Once he got out he started again and with each success got bolder and bolder."

"So if he'd left Louisville, you'd still be in prison?"

He quaked. "Yes. For life."

"Are the memories of your family haunting you?"

"Yes."

She attempted to stand, swayed and grabbed the railing, her hand next to his. "I know how that is. If you allow memories to, they can take over your life."

He hadn't thought it possible to tighten his hold on the wood railing, but he did. "I should have been there. Then they might be alive. But I was too busy working!"

"So even though you are free now, you really aren't. You're living in a self-imposed prison, the bars as strong as if they were made of steel."

"You sound like you speak from experience."

"I've been there. Probably still am. I know what guilt can do to a person. Don't you think I've beat myself up over the fact that Tom needed help and I didn't see it? I was too busy trying to deal with Crystal's accident and getting her well. My husband needed me."

Her words came to a quavering stop. He wanted to hold her, take her pain away, but he didn't have the right. In fact, after this evening she probably wouldn't want to have anything to do with him. He would remind her of Tom every time she saw him.

"I wasn't there for him, and when he was sent to prison, he rejected any help I tried to give him. My concern was too late and he made it clear he wanted nothing to do with his family." Tanya released a long breath. "I could understand his feelings toward me, but not his daughter. It tore Crystal up that she couldn't see her father."

"Prison isn't any place to have a family reunion."

She thrust her face toward him. "You sound like Tom! I married him for better or worse, and he discarded me when things got bad." Her voice rose several levels.

Knowing he would provoke her further, Chance inched closer until their breaths tangled. "Do you blame Tom?"

"Yes!" Tanya shouted then immediately covered her mouth, stepping back until the pool of light revealed the shock on her face.

For a few more seconds she continued to stare at Chance, then she whirled and fled into the house. The slamming of the door reverberated in the stillness and shuddered down his length. His legs weak, he fell back onto the step. He sat there in the dark and watched one light after another go out in the house. Minutes ticked into thirty and still he couldn't move.

What had he done? What can of worms had he opened with his confession? With no lease to protect him, he could be asked to leave tomorrow morning, then where would he be with his promise to himself?

All energy siphoned from him, he rested his elbows on his knees and clasped his hands together. He stared into the blackness of the night and wished he could erase the past hour. He hadn't wanted her to find out from someone else about his past, but the truth was he hadn't wanted her to know at all. How was he going to put it behind him when every time he saw her he would think of this evening?

Lord, where are You?

Chapter Five

❧

Lord, where are You?

Tanya sat in the dark in her bedroom, aware that Chance was still out on the stairs to his apartment. She had seen him through the slats in her blinds and for a fleeting moment she had wanted to go out and take him into her arms to ease his hurt.

I need You, God. I don't know what to feel.

After the initial shock had worn off, anger had taken hold of her until she had heard his story. How could she not feel his pain as he had spoken about his murdered wife and daughter?

But how can I help him, Lord? You ask too much of me.

The remnants of her life were held together with a glue that threatened to dissolve at the least little problem. She was a stronger person than she had been this time last year, but not this strong—to help someone discover God's love and mercy. *I just can't. I don't have what it takes.*

She lay down and turned onto her side, staring at the thin slivers of light pushing their way through the slats of the blinds. He was still out there—hurting, confused. She didn't have to get up and look. She felt it in her heart.

Squeezing her eyes closed, she hoped to block the lone image of Chance that haunted her. She couldn't. He loomed before her, materializing on the black screen of her mind with that half grin on his mouth while his eyes were full of pain.

She twisted to her other side and pounded her pillow. It didn't do any good. Frustration clutched her in a viselike grip.

She wasn't going to have any peace until she answered God's call. *You don't realize what You're asking! I could do more harm than good.*

As she settled back on the pillow and peered up at the ceiling, she resolved to be there for Chance. She would do the best she could and prayed God would be with her every step of the way with Chance.

At a few minutes before seven Chance rang Tanya's doorbell. A long moment passed. He turned to leave, part of him surprised that Tanya wouldn't keep her jogging date with him. But the other part wasn't. Not after the night before. Not after he had told her about his past.

His foot was on the first step when the door swung open. He spun around and faced Tanya, flustered, flushed.

"Sorry, I was late getting home. I just flew in the door a couple of minutes ago and threw on these pants and T-shirt." She came out onto the porch and sat on the step to finish tying one of her sneakers. When she rose, she gave him a sheepish look. "You think this is okay for jogging?"

Chance allowed his gaze to roam slowly down the length of Tanya, dressed in the bottom half of a bright pink jogging suit with the price tag still on it and an old, several sizes too large, white T-shirt. "You look fine."

More than fine, he thought but kept that to himself. Patches of red colored Tanya's cheeks, giving her a fresh, appealing look. Although she had been through a lot, there was still a touch of innocence about her.

"What do we do first? Stretch? Run in place?"

Her large eyes charmed him. For a long moment until a little frown wrinkled her forehead, he was so entranced by her mahogany gaze, he didn't realize she had spoken. Turning away, he broke her spell, appalled that he had been caught staring at her, and said, "First, let's take this off."

As he pointed toward the price tag, her gasp of surprise sounded, followed by her laughter. "I told you I was in a hurry. I didn't have anything to jog in so I got this on my way home from work. Now that I've spent my hard-earned money, I'm committed to doing this." With a tug, she ripped the tag off and stuffed it into her pocket. "Ready."

"I always do better if I stretch first."

As Chance went through a series of stretches, Tanya followed suit. Then he set off at a slow jog down Berryhill Road toward the lake. His sneakers pounded the pavement in rhythm with Tanya's. Their synchronized pace made him yearn for a time when Tom didn't stand between them, and yet her late husband was the very reason he was in Sweetwater.

When the lake came into view, Chance found the path that edged the shoreline, often used by joggers. He headed west, the sun below the line of trees, streaks of rose, orange and light pink fingering upward.

"Doing okay?" he asked after ten minutes.

Between pants, Tanya answered, "I…think… so."

Another ten minutes and Chance slowed to

a walk. "Let's go to the boulder up ahead then turn back."

She didn't reply for twenty seconds then said, "Fine."

Chance slid a glance at her face, noting the sheen of sweat glistening on her forehead, her flushed cheeks. "Or, we can stop and rest if you want."

Her gaze swept to his. "No." She inhaled and exhaled shallow breaths. "I can do this."

At the boulder he started back the way they had come and noticed Tanya's breathing was more even and the red patches were fading from her cheeks. Even though he hadn't been jogging for long, he had been in shape before this. He suspected Tanya wasn't. He shouldn't have pushed so hard earlier. He would remember next time—if there was a next time. They still needed to talk about the evening before.

He came to a place in the path only five feet from the shoreline of the lake and stopped. "We've done enough for the first day. Let's rest, then walk back at a more leisurely pace. This is a beautiful spot." He saw some huge flat rocks not far away, crossed to the first one and sat, facing the water.

Tanya stayed on the trail for a moment. If

the hairs tingling on his neck were any indication, she was staring at him and trying to decide what to do.

Without looking back at her, he said, "I haven't gotten to enjoy something like this in a long time."

Her sigh drifted to him, then the sound of her footsteps as she made her way to the rock next to his. She lowered herself onto it and brought her legs up to clasp them. Keeping her head averted, she stared at the water.

"Beautiful, isn't it?" he asked to break the silence.

She nodded.

The gentle lapping of the water and the colors of the sunset reflected in the lake soothed him for the few minutes he allowed to pass before he broached the subject of last night. "Do you want me to stay in the apartment? I'll leave if I make you uncomfortable. That isn't what I intended."

Finally she looked at him. "What *did* you intend?"

"To tell you the truth. To tell you about the time I spent in prison."

"With Tom?"

"Yeah."

Peering away, she sighed. "I need the rent and

I think you need a place to stay, so no, I don't want you to move."

"I didn't want you to hear about it from someone else."

"Like Samuel?"

"He wouldn't have told you. He told me that first day in Sweetwater it was my story to tell."

Tanya grinned. "That sounds like Samuel. But I'm guessing he made it clear you should tell me as quickly as you could."

"Yep. That's Samuel for you. He has this way of manipulating you into doing what he thinks should be done."

"But you aren't attending church." She swung fully around so she faced Chance. "I know he's tried because Samuel wouldn't be Samuel unless he did."

Chance nodded.

"But because of what happened to you, you think God has abandoned you?"

"That about sums it up. Ruth was a devout Christian and look what happened to her."

"The Lord never promised us a bed of roses—at least not on Earth. He hasn't abandoned you. He's waiting for you to return to Him."

"I doubt it," Chance mumbled, pushing off the rock. He stood in front of Tanya, holding out his hand to her. "Ready to head back? We'll walk slowly."

In other words, the subject is off-limits, Tanya thought, and fit her hand in his. His touch warmed her fingers as the air began to chill with the approach of night. She shivered.

"Cold?"

"I think the heat wave has broken. This morning it was a nice fifty-five degrees when I went to work."

He inhaled. "Fall is finally in the air. About time. It'll be October in a few days."

Tanya fell into step next to him on the path. "I love fall. That means winter is right around the corner. The holidays. The cold weather."

"I'll like the cold weather, but the holidays..." His voice faded into the silence, some insects serenading the only sound heard.

That shadow passed over his features, the one that meant he was remembering a time when life had been good, then was snatched away. "I didn't put up the outdoor decorations last year, but maybe this year." With Tom's imprisonment she and Crystal hadn't felt very festive the past few years, but Chance needed to laugh again, to be a part of a family, a community.

"I used to do that," Chance finally said a

couple of minutes later. "And when it snowed, my daughter used—" He swallowed hard, coming to a halt in the middle of the path.

Tanya turned back toward him. "You should talk about Haley. She hasn't left you. She's in here." Boldly she laid her hand over his heart and felt its pounding beneath her palm—strong, a bit too fast.

He covered her hand, then pulled it away but didn't release it. "Those memories are the only thing in prison that kept me sane at times."

"I know. The thought of Crystal has been what has kept me going these past few years. She needs me. I can't let her down."

His other hand came up to cup hers between his. "You aren't. You're doing a good job with Crystal."

The dark shadows crept closer as night approached. Tanya relished his nearness for a moment before she realized the danger in that. Neither one of them was ready for anything serious and that was all she thought about as his hands held hers. Reluctantly she pulled away, breaking their physical contact.

"Not good enough. I still don't know what's bothering Crystal. She won't talk to me about it."

"She's fifteen. She'll come around. You two have a good relationship. Did you find out anything about someone harassing her at school?"

"Not yet. Beth is looking into it for me since Crystal's in her class."

"If I can help, I will." He started walking toward the street that was lit a hundred yards away.

"You've done so much in the short time you've been here. All Crystal has been talking about is basketball since you put up that hoop. I wish I had a sports wheelchair for her. The electric one is great for getting around school and especially any large place, but when it comes to doing something like shooting baskets, it isn't as effective."

"She's adapting."

"That's my daughter. She has always been so upbeat until Tom died. His death really took a toll on her. For the first time she didn't confide in me and since then, she has drawn more and more inside herself." *Much like you,* Tanya thought, slanting a look at Chance, illuminated in the streetlight as they stepped onto the pavement.

"Has she talked to Samuel about her father's death?"

"Yes, but I don't think she was too open even with him. He told me to give her time. I know time helps us sees things in a different light, but I'm her mother and hate seeing her suffer."

Chance's expression tightened into a frown. "It's hard for a parent to watch his child hurting."

"Sometimes I wonder if life will ever get any easier. There's always something, but then I'm fortunate. I have a home, my faith, a loving daughter and wonderful friends."

"I guess if life was too easy we would get bored and complacent."

"It keeps us on our toes?"

"Yeah, something like that." Chance crossed the street and turned down Berryhill Road. "Think you can jog the rest of the way?"

"That's what I'm here for." She took off for her house, pushing herself as her long legs chewed up the length to her yard.

She heard Chance's chuckle echo in the night, then the pounding of his footsteps behind her. Out of the corner of her eye, she saw him pull alongside her, nod his head then pass her. The rest of the way she watched his back, proud that she was able to keep up the pace for the most part even though her lungs burned and her muscles protested the unusual exertion.

"The Last Chance Picnic at the beginning of November is only a week away," Zoey said as she slid into the booth at Alice's Café.

Tanya scooted over as she saw Beth enter

the restaurant, the last to arrive for their usual Saturday morning get-together. The concern on her friend's face alerted Tanya that something was wrong. "What happened?"

"I'm hungry." Beth unwrapped her silverware and placed her paper napkin in her lap. "I wonder if Alice has her pecan pies made yet. I sure could use a slice."

"Okay, Beth Morgan, what's going on?" Jesse signaled for Alice to take their orders.

Beth didn't say anything until after they had all given the café owner their orders, then she drew in a deep breath and released it on a long sigh. "Some people make me so angry!"

Surprised by her fervent tone, Tanya asked, "Who made you angry?"

"Felicia. I dropped Allie off at the library to help Felicia with story time and she just had to fill my ears with lies."

Darcy shifted on the chair at the end of the booth, her brows crunching together. "What lies?"

"About Chance. She had the nerve to tell me he had been in prison for murder. If that were true, he would still be there. Why does she love to spread—"

"It's true, Beth," Tanya said and held her breath as the implication of her words sank in with each of her friends. She thought she had heard something at the bank with one of her co-workers yesterday, but when she had joined the others, the woman had changed the subject.

Her mouth hung open for a few seconds before Beth asked, "Murder! Is that where Samuel knew him? From prison?"

"Yes—"

"Is he out on parole? How many years did he serve?" Jesse leaned forward.

Alice brought their drinks, and Tanya waited until she left to reply, "The real killer was caught and he petitioned the court to have the conviction overturned, which it was. So technically he was in prison for murder, but he didn't do it. The man who did is awaiting trial."

"How horrible." Jesse covered her mouth.

"What's worse is someone is spreading false rumors about Chance." Beth dumped more sugar than usual into her coffee and stirred so hard that it sloshed over onto the table.

"You know how it is. Someone hears a story, alters it a little when he retells it and before long a person can't recognize what the original story was." Zoey sipped her hot tea.

"I don't want Chance to suffer anymore. He's gone through enough with the murders of his wife and daughter—"

"That's who he was accused of killing?" Darcy asked, pushing herself to her feet and stretching. "Ooh, my back is really hurting."

"It won't be long," Jesse said, patting her hand, then looked at Tanya. "Was it his wife and daughter?"

Tanya nodded, remembering the night four weeks before when he'd told her that. She hurt for him. In the time since then, they'd jogged together several evenings a week, and he had joined her and Crystal for dinner a few nights then helped her daughter with shooting baskets or just talked with them on the deck. But in all that time they had spent together, there was a reserve between them, put there by what he'd shared with her that night.

Jesse clenched her hand on the table. "No one better say anything to me. He works for Nick. He's part of our family now. Nick has really been impressed with Chance's work. Usually Nick has to travel frequently to Chicago, and would have this week, but he sent Chance and he did a great job."

Tanya had heard a car dropping Chance off late the night before. She hadn't been able to go to sleep until she had known he'd returned from Chicago safely. She hadn't seen him in three days, fifteen hours, but then who was counting? Okay, she missed seeing him, even if it was only long enough to wave and say hi. She liked knowing he was nearby.

"Yeah, Dane says he's really helping with setting up the financial records for the youth center. Accounting isn't my husband's strong suit." Zoey took the plate that Alice handed her with a piece of spinach and bacon quiche.

Alice served the rest of them, then said, "Are you talking about Chance Taylor?"

Tanya stiffened, the hand holding her fork tightening. "Yes, we were."

"I heard something troubling yesterday morning. Almost said something to you when you came in, Tanya, with him being your tenant and all, but I didn't get an opportunity. He was in prison for murder. Did you know that?"

The dismay on Alice's face knotted Tanya's stomach. "I knew, and the conviction was overturned. He is innocent."

"He is? Are you sure? Wilbur said he read an article online about Chance. He went to prison for murdering his family!"

Tanya narrowed her eyes, ready to stand on the table and shout the truth to the whole café. "I'm sure. If you don't believe me, Alice, ask Samuel. He knows the truth."

"Or you can ask my husband," Jesse added,

tension in her voice. "Nick would never hire someone he hadn't thoroughly checked out. He would never invite someone to his house for dinner with his family if he was a murderer."

"I guess you're right. If I hear someone talking about it, I'll tell them they're wrong." Alice hurried away.

"I've never seen Alice move so fast. I think we scared her," Darcy said, rubbing her lower back.

"At least she got the point Chance is innocent and won't be contributing to the wrong gossip spreading." Tanya forced herself to relax back against the leather cushioned booth. "By the way, Jesse, what dinner with your family?" Thinking back over the past four weeks, surprisingly she could account for Chance's whereabouts in the evenings—even when he wasn't with her and Crystal.

"The one I'm having tomorrow evening. I don't want to be accused of lying. I'll call him and ask him over. Why don't you and Crystal come, too, so he'll feel more comfortable eating with the boss's family?"

Darcy laughed. "Watch out, Tanya. She's at it again."

A few weeks ago she would have panicked over the idea that Jesse was doing her matchmaking thing with her. But after not seeing Chance for almost four days, Tanya would be glad to accompany him to dinner at Jesse and Nick's. "We'll be there. That is, if Chance says yes."

Jesse smiled. "I know you can persuade him. It can't hurt for the town to see we believe in him."

"No," Beth said. "I'll make sure Samuel is aware of what's happening, but he probably has already heard the rumors, knowing my husband."

"Well, I've got a piece of news he probably hasn't heard yet." Jesse glanced at each one at the table, then said, "I'm going to have a baby in seven months!"

"Oh, good, you can experience what I've been experiencing for the past seven months." Darcy rose. "I'm so happy for you. Be back in a sec." She hastened toward the restroom.

"Congratulations. I didn't know you and Nick were trying," Zoey said.

"We weren't exactly, but it's great news. We're happy. That's one of the reasons we're so glad Chance is doing such a good job. It'll give Nick more time when the baby comes."

Tanya wondered if Chance would stick around that long. She wasn't sure he wanted to settle in Sweetwater permanently. She got the feeling coming to town was just a temporary thing for him. And now with the rumors flying around Sweetwater, he might not stay past the weekend. She would have to tell him. She didn't want him to find out when someone asked him about being in prison or snubbed him.

That evening Tanya stepped out onto the deck and looked toward the apartment above her garage. The fall air held a crispness, mingled with the scents of burning leaves and wood. The sun's rays peeked over the treetops to the west, streaks of pinks and oranges coloring the pale blue sky. A beautiful day. Not the kind of day to tell a man she cared about that the town knew about the time he had spent in prison.

She backed up until she pressed against the door into her house. Thoughts of escaping inside and not saying anything to Chance dominated her mind. With trembling hands, she pushed herself away from the door and strode toward the stairs that led to his apartment.

She couldn't do that to him. He deserved better than that. She could imagine him walking into a room where everyone stopped talking at once and stared at him. It had happened to her on a number of occasions a few years ago until Darcy, Jesse, Beth and Zoey had rallied around her and supported her through that dark time. Finally the rumors had died down and people had ceased speculating if she had known about her husband's activities. She'd guessed the townspeople had decided if her friends accepted that she hadn't known, then they could, too, especially when Tom had set fire to a barn that Darcy had been trapped in. But it had hurt that the people hadn't believed in her at first. She had lived in Sweetwater most of her life. They should have known she hadn't been aware.

At the bottom of the steps, Tanya paused and peered at the door above. He was in there. She had seen him come home with several bags of groceries while she had been cleaning the kitchen and occasionally staring out the window at the driveway where he would have to pass in order to get to his apartment. That had been twenty minutes ago, and it had taken her that amount of time to get up her courage to see him.

First one foot then the other settled on the steps. She gripped the railing, then hurried up before she changed her mind—again. Fortifying herself with a deep breath, she rapped on the door. She kept her hand clenched even when she dropped it to her side to stay the trembling.

Chance opened the door. A smile moved

across his mouth, slow and full with his dimples appearing. His eyes lit with warmth. "Hi, what brings you by?"

That was a perfect opening to tell him why she had come to see him. Instead, she returned his smile, the corners of her mouth quivering slightly. "How did your trip go?"

She walked inside as he held the door open. She hadn't been in his apartment in several weeks and noticed a few changes, a couple of personal touches added—a clock, a radio, a book on the table, a photo of a beautiful woman and a young girl who had to be his daughter. Tanya saw the resemblance in the smile, the eyes, the dark hair.

"I accomplished what Nick needed done."

"Then it was successful. Great!" Even to her own ears, her voice sounded strained, a little high-pitched.

Chance studied her with narrowed eyes. "Is something wrong? Is it Crystal?"

Waving her hand, Tanya twisted away from his too-perceptive gaze. "No. No, she's fine. Well, at least okay. On Thursday I think something happened at school. She came home in a bad mood and didn't say a word the whole evening. She didn't leave her bedroom except to eat dinner. She would have eaten that in her room, but I wouldn't let her."

"Has Beth discovered anything at school?" Chance moved into her line of vision.

She couldn't turn away this time. His gaze captured hers and held it. "Only what I told you before you left. There are a couple of girls she noticed talking to Crystal in the hallway last week. Afterward Crystal went into the restroom and was late for class. It looked like she had been crying, but Beth couldn't get anything out of Crystal. She sent her to Zoey, but she couldn't, either. My daughter isn't talking."

"I'll try again to see if I can find out anything. That is, if you don't mind."

"No, please try. For the longest time I wouldn't ask for help when I needed it. I've learned to now. We all need help from time to time, and there's nothing wrong in admitting that." She moistened her lips and decided the time had come. "With that in mind, Chance, I need to tell you there are some rumors going around about you having been in prison for murder."

For a second nothing registered on his expression, then it went blank as though he had completely shut down his emotions. "I figured it would be only a matter of time before someone would get wind of it. In a few months the trial of my family's killer will be all over the media in Louisville. What happened to me will come up."

"And you'll have to relive the horror all over again." She took a step closer, half afraid he would distance himself from her.

He held his ground, sadness leaking into his expression. "Yes."

"I want you to know I'll help you any way I can. So will Darcy, Zoey, Beth and Jesse. In fact, Jesse wants us to come over to dinner tomorrow night."

"I don't think—"

"She's the boss's wife. You can't say no, Chance. Besides, you can't stay holed up in here. You need to get out and let everyone know what they are saying doesn't bother you."

His half grin returned. "Who said I was gonna stay holed up in my apartment? I could have plans already."

"I just assumed—I mean—" she said, flustered. Had he met someone? The thought bothered her, for some reason.

His laughter filled the room. "Sorry. I couldn't resist. I don't have any plans. I'm gonna work at the youth center in the afternoon, but I can be ready to go. What time tomorrow?"

"Six."

"Speaking of the youth center, does Crystal ever go?"

"She hasn't yet."

"Do you think she would like to go tomorrow while I'm there? The art teacher from school is going to have a class tomorrow afternoon. I thought she might like to sit in on it since she hasn't had a chance to take art at school yet."

"I'll say something to her. If she wants to, I can drop you two off."

He covered the space between them, only a foot separating them. "You could give a class in drawing people for the kids. Dane's always looking for people to do classes that might interest the teens."

She backed away. "No. I can't teach." Her legs hit a chair, and she stopped. "I'll leave that to others."

"You've taught Crystal a lot. She's very talented. Like you."

"I merely showed her how to use her natural talent. That's not teaching."

"I beg your pardon. That *is* teaching. A teacher shows a person how to tap into his talent."

Chance shrank the space between them, his familiar scent of springtime soap drifting to her. "Don't sell yourself short. Share your talent with others."

Tanya sidestepped away and headed for the

door. "I'll talk to Crystal and let you know tomorrow. I'm glad you're back." She hurried from his apartment.

Chance went to the window and watched Tanya's flight down the stairs and across the driveway. He lost sight of her, but he didn't need to see her to know every minute detail of her beautiful face—a face he had pictured more than once while he was in Chicago these past few days. When had his feelings changed toward Tanya? She was no longer just someone he had promised himself he would help, then move on. She was more. And there was no way he would allow himself to become involved with Tom's wife. How could he when he was the reason Tom was dead in the first place as though he had plunged the knife into Tom's heart himself?

Turning away from the window, Chance took in his new home, a home that was now invaded by his past. He'd known it would come out. He had just hoped he would have had more time in Sweetwater. He didn't know if he could stay and face the townspeople each day, knowing what they were thinking: did the authorities really have the right man this time?

Chance closed the program on the computer, having finished putting in the numbers for

October. The simple accounting for the youth center was the closest he would be to his old life as a financial advisor. He wanted nothing to do with that life. He dreaded the time he would have to return to Louisville for the trial of his wife and daughter's murderer. He couldn't even bring himself to say the man's name.

"Oh, good. You haven't left yet," Dane said from the doorway into the office at the center.

Chance glanced up. "I'll be leaving as soon as the art class is over. What do you need?"

Dane moved into the office, perching on the side of the desk. "I don't need anything. Just wanted to see if there was anything I could do for you. You've been a blessing to us here."

Chance couldn't keep the skepticism from his expression. "Keeping the books isn't difficult. I'm sure you would have found someone to do it."

"But you saved me having to appeal to others. You stepped forward."

"Samuel has a way of persuading a person to do things."

"Yeah, he does. He's one of the reasons I'm running this place." Dane folded his arms over his chest and looked as if he were there for the long haul.

Chance's wariness tingled along his neck. "You've heard?"

"Yes, a couple of days ago my neighbor, Wilbur Thompson, wanted me to know about the kind of person I let volunteer at the youth center."

"If you don't want me to—"

Dane's eyebrows slashed downward. "I will never let Wilbur tell me what I can and can't do. We have a long history. We've come to a precarious truce since we live on the same short block and go to the same church." The anger in his expression dissolved. "I'm telling you this because I want you to know you are welcome here for as long as you want to volunteer."

"You don't have any questions?"

"About what?"

"Like did I really do it?"

Thunder lined Dane's face. "The system isn't always perfect. Occasionally the police are wrong, but thankfully they discovered their mistake and corrected it. The man I've become acquainted with this past month couldn't have done that to his family."

Chance closed his eyes, relieved to hear those words from a man he respected. He knew that Dane Witherspoon had once been in law enforcement and for him to say that meant a lot to him. "Thank you. I've come to enjoy my time spent at the center. I was gonna offer to tutor some of the kids in math if you need someone."

"Do I ever! Math isn't my strength. Now that school is underway, I'm getting some requests from the teens for different tutors to help them in their schoolwork. Math tops the list. In fact, Holly Proctor and Eddy O'Neal have asked me on more than one occasion. Let me talk with them and see if we can set something up several evenings a week. When could you do it?"

"I'm free any evening." Chance realized except for going to work and seeing Tanya and Crystal from time to time, his life was spent in his apartment reading, listening to the radio and thinking. He had too much free time on his hands. "Just let me know when to be here. I'm getting a cell phone this week so you will have a way of getting hold of me besides calling work or Tanya."

"What's next? A car?"

Chance shrugged. "It's been easy getting around Sweetwater, but I guess I'll have to get one in the near future." He thought about the time when he would have to return to Louisville. It would be easier if he had his own transportation by then.

"Let me know. I might be able to help you with getting a reliable used car."

Chance rose, his muscles tight from sitting for so long. He stretched then rolled his head around to ease the tension in his neck and shoulders. "Thanks. If you hear of anything, let me know. I can't afford much."

"You have a good job. You could get a loan."

He shook his head. "No. I don't want any debt to tie me down to material things." That was one of the reasons he had worked so long and hard before. He'd had debts to pay from accumulating a large house, two brand-new cars and some of the latest electronic devices. It had all come tumbling down around him, leaving him with nothing. Never again.

Dane pushed off the desk and walked toward the door. "That's not a bad philosophy. Pay as you go. With three children that's getting to be harder and harder."

Chance followed Dane from the office, intending to find Crystal and see if she was through with her art class. Dane headed toward the gym while he went in the opposite direction toward the hallway that led to the six rooms used for various activities like classes, counseling sessions and meetings.

When he popped his head into the room used

for the art class, he only noticed the teacher and a young man left. "Do you know where Crystal Bolton is?"

"She left a few minutes ago with a couple of the girls. She shouldn't be too far," the art teacher said.

Chance retraced his steps and peered into the gym then the exercise room but didn't see Crystal. Would she have gone home without letting him know? Even if she had left, Tanya would have let him know she was taking her daughter home. So where was Crystal?

He went back to the six rooms and began to check each one. Two teenage girls came out of the last one on the right, the TV room, giggling and whispering to themselves. One hugged a sketchbook to her chest. When they saw him, they stopped talking and quickened their pace and passed him. The teen with the sketchbook tossed it on the floor halfway down the hall.

An uneasiness gripped him. Crystal's sketchbook lay discarded, opened to the page of the young boy she had a crush on.

The beating of his heart slowed for a few seconds then slammed against his rib cage. He hastened toward the last door on the right, his gut clenched into a huge knot. Just inside he found Crystal on the floor, sobbing.

Chapter Six

The sobs wrenched Chance's soul, squeezing his heart, prodding him into action. He crossed the room and knelt next to Crystal, sprawled on the floor by her wheelchair, her body shaking with her cries.

He touched her shoulder. "Crystal, are you hurt?"

"Go away. Leave—me alone," she said between her sobs, her face buried in her hands.

For a flash he pictured his daughter on the floor, crying as though the world had come to an end. And he hadn't thought it possible for his heart to hurt any more but it did. "I'm not leaving. You're stuck with me. Are you hurt?" He schooled his voice to an even level, calm, soothing.

She quieted but didn't say anything.

"Should I call your mother and have her come pick us up?"

She twisted her upper body until she glared up at him. "No!"

"I'm going to help you into your wheelchair and then you and I are going to talk." Again he made sure his voice betrayed none of the anger quickly coming to the foreground within him as he stared at her pale face, streaked with tears.

Her glare intensified, but Chance ignored it as he gathered her into his arms and hoisted her up. After securing her in her wheelchair, he backed up and sat on the couch a few feet away. His own body shook with anger that he was no longer able to suppress. Those two girls leaving the room had been responsible for Crystal lying on the floor crying. It took all his control not to storm after the two teens and demand an explanation then an apology to Crystal.

"What happened?" Chance leaned forward, resting his elbows on his thighs.

She dropped her head, staring at her hands clasped together in her lap.

"Crystal, I saw two girls leaving the room. Do you want me to go and ask them? Because one way or another, I will find out what happened."

Her head snapped up. "No! Don't!" Panic thundered in her voice.

"Then talk to me. I want to help."

"You can't. No one can." The panic slid into defeat. Her shoulders hunched over, and she returned to staring at her hands.

"I didn't tell you before, but now that some people know I figure you should hear it from me. Up until a couple of months ago I was in prison for a crime I didn't commit. They found the real killer and my conviction was overturned." When he had mentioned prison, Crystal's clasp tightened until her knuckles were white. "I knew your father. He was my friend."

Crystal raised her head and looked at him, her eyes glistening. "Dad? I—I—" She cleared her throat. "He wouldn't see me. Why?"

"Because he hated what he had done, what he had become. He didn't want you to remember him behind bars. He loved you so much he only wanted you to remember the good times you all had."

A tear slipped from her eye and rolled down her cheek. "He loved me?"

"He talked about you all the time. Believe me, Crystal, he loved you very much." Her tears produced a constriction in his throat. "I'm telling you about my time in prison because it was your father who helped me deal with some prisoners who liked to bully the new person. I learned quick to stand up for myself. You have to stand up for yourself and let these girls know what they are doing isn't going to get to you."

"But it does."

"Then don't let them see that. A bully feeds off others' fears and weaknesses."

"But look at me. How can I fight back?" Crystal scrubbed a hand across her cheeks.

"By believing in yourself. You are a beautiful, talented young lady who happens to be in a wheelchair. We all have issues we have to deal with, even those two girls."

"But still—"

"Start with your friends. Let them know exactly what is going on. Let them help you. That even includes your mother. You aren't alone. Believe it or not, those girls are the ones with the problem. They feel belittling you makes them important."

Crystal sniffled, blinking away the remaining tears in her eyes. "Mom will want to say something to them. I can't tell her."

"She's very concerned about you. She knows someone is bothering you. Please let her help by listening to you."

"I have to deal with them on my own. I can't let my mother stand up for me. That will only make it worse."

"Maybe. But being silent about being harassed won't solve the problem, either. Think about what I've said, and remember if you need someone to talk to, I'm here for you, as is your mother." Chance rose. "Now, do you still want to walk home? Or do you want me to call your mother to come pick us up?"

Crystal drew in a shuddering breath. "I need some time. Let's walk."

"Well, we couldn't have asked for a better afternoon. It's beautiful outside." He started for the door.

"I need you to switch my battery on. One of them turned it off so I couldn't go anywhere in my chair. They took my sketchbook and were taunting me with it. They said I had to reach for it. I tried but leaned too far and fell. They left laughing and giggling. They took it with them."

"No, they didn't. They threw it down in the hallway as they came out of the room. We'll get it when we leave." Chance went behind Crystal and flipped the switch on the battery. "You're all set. Let's go. I need some fresh air."

The walls seemed to be closing in on him. All the memories of the bullies he'd handled in prison inundated him, underscoring the uphill battle Crystal had in her own situation. He dragged in deep breaths to alleviate the pressure in his chest as he left the TV room.

In the hallway Chance picked up the sketchbook and gave it to Crystal, glad to see it wasn't damaged. A few minutes later they were on the street and heading toward Berryhill Road. A crisp breeze and the exertion of walking cooled Chance's anger and eased the suffocating sensation the incident with Crystal had produced. He had dealt with bullies in prison, but why did someone like Tanya's daughter have to?

Why aren't You helping her, God? Crystal doesn't deserve this on top of everything else that has happened to her in the past four years. Where is Your love?

As they neared home, Crystal said, "Don't say anything to Mom, please."

"I can't lie to her, but I won't say anything to her. You need to tell her, though."

"She's been through so much."

"She's strong, Crystal. She doesn't need protecting."

"You haven't been here. She's—" She snapped her mouth closed.

"I know she is bipolar. Your dad told me."

"Then you understand it's been tough for her. I don't want to add to her problems. She's had to deal with so many."

"Not saying anything makes the situation worse for your mother. She is imagining all kinds of things. The truth will be hard, but not as hard as what she can think of."

The front door opened and Tanya came out onto the porch, waving to them as they came up the driveway. She descended the steps and walked to them. "How did it go? Did you enjoy the art lesson?"

Crystal pasted a bright smile on her face. "It was great. I want to take art next year under Mrs. Garrison."

"We have about an hour before we need to get ready for dinner at Jesse and Nick's." Tanya glanced at Chance and noticed a tightness about his mouth and wondered what had put it there. Had someone said something to him about being in prison?

"I'll be ready," Crystal said, heading to the ramp in back.

Chance started for his apartment.

"Did something happen at the center?"

With his back to her, he stiffened. "What do you mean?"

He didn't turn around, but Tanya didn't have to see his face to know something had gone wrong. She heard it in the clipped edge to his voice. "Did someone say something to you about your past?"

"No, not really." The tenseness in his shoulders eased. "Dane and I talked some about what he'd heard. He wanted me to know he stood behind me."

"Then what happened?"

Slowly he pivoted. "You need to talk to your daughter. I promised Crystal I wouldn't say anything."

She gritted her teeth and strode to him. "What happened? Tell me."

"I can't break a promise to Crystal. Don't ask me to."

Anger surged through her. Her fingernails dug into her palms. "You shouldn't have promised her."

"She thinks she's protecting you. Go talk to her."

"I *have* talked to her." His words cut deep into her. Crystal had always tried to protect her and at one time she had needed that. But not now.

"After today, maybe she's ready." Chance resumed his steps toward his apartment.

Tanya watched him climb the stairs, trying desperately to tamp down her irritation at Chance's silence. She thought about following him and demanding he break his promise to her daughter but knew his integrity wouldn't allow it. Instead, she spun about and hurried into her house to find her daughter. What had happened to put such a hard edge into Chance's voice? She knew how cruel some kids could be, and she didn't want what she was thinking to be true. She didn't want her daughter to go through that kind of pain.

When is it enough, Lord? She's suffered enough. Help me!

At her daughter's bedroom door, she knocked. "Yes?"

"We should talk, Crystal."

The sound of the wheelchair moving toward the door came through the wood. Tanya released the breath she had been holding when she realized her daughter wasn't going to shut her out—at least, not physically.

When Crystal maneuvered her chair so Tanya could enter the bedroom, her daughter asked, "What did Chance tell you?" Tension lined her face, and she appeared ten years older.

"Absolutely nothing and that's the problem. He wouldn't tell me anything, but I know something happened this afternoon at the center."

Her expression relaxed into a bland one. "Not much. I took an art lesson."

"Crystal, please don't shut me out anymore. I'm going crazy trying to figure out what's going on with you. I know you're hurting. Let me help you."

"You've got your own problems, Mom. I can take care of this by myself."

"But you don't have to. I can help. That's what family is for. To help each other." Tanya sank onto her daughter's bed, the ice-green sheets crumpled at the foot of it. She plucked at the cotton material. "Did someone bother you today?"

Crystal swiveled her chair around so she faced her desk with her outdated computer.

"Darling, you're scaring me."

The fear in Tanya's voice must have conveyed her concern more than her words because her daughter peered over her shoulder, sadness in her eyes, as she asked, "If I tell you, will you promise to let me deal with it?"

Tanya scooted to the edge of the bed, her hands gripping the bedding. "I will for as long as I can, but if you can't take care of it by yourself, I will step in. I have to. I'm your mother. That's all I can promise you."

Her daughter swung her wheelchair back around. With a deep sigh, she said, "Two girls took my sketchbook and taunted me with it.

When I reached for it, I fell out of my chair. They left, laughing. That's when Chance came in."

Tanya tried to control her reaction to her child's words, but it seeped through her restraint. In Crystal's mirror over her dresser Tanya saw in her expression the shock, hurt and anger all tangled together, flashing in and out so fast they collided with each other. Finally she schooled her features into a look that didn't convey pity or rage. Her daughter wouldn't accept either of those, she instinctively realized.

"What did Chance do?" Only the last word quavered with the emotions she quelled.

"Picked me up and helped me back into the wheelchair."

"You aren't hurt?"

"Only my ego. I knew when I went into the room with them they were up to no good, but they snatched my sketchbook when I came into the hall after class. I reacted without really thinking. I won't do that again."

Her daughter shouldn't have to worry about something like that! "Who are the girls?"

"Just two sophomores. I don't want to talk about them anymore. I've let them ruin enough of my day." Crystal tilted her head to the side. "Aren't we going to Jesse and Nick's tonight? You aren't wearing that, are you?"

Tanya glanced down at her worn jeans with several holes in them. "I thought this was what all the teens like to wear." Her cleaning attire with her oversize T-shirt was only worn at home.

"Yeah. Some even buy brand-new ones with holes already in them. But, Mom, you're too—"

Tanya held up her hand to stop her child's words. "Don't you say I'm too old to. I'm changing, but only because I was anyway." She infused a lightness into her voice. "We'll leave in about half an hour." She pushed herself off the bed and strode toward the door. Before leaving, she added, "You aren't alone, honey. Remember that, if things get too hard to handle on your own."

When she left her daughter's bedroom, Tanya didn't go into hers. Instead, she headed toward the kitchen and paced its small confines, peeking out the window with each pass at the stairs that led to Chance's. Chewing on her fingernail, she debated whether to pay him a visit or not. There were details she wanted to know.

Finally ten minutes later, she made her way to his apartment. But before she could knock, the door swung open. He stepped to the side to allow her inside.

"Is Crystal okay?" Chance asked as he faced her.

"Yes—no. She said she was physically fine,

but this incident really hurt her." Tanya paced from the kitchen table to the couch, then back. "How can I make this go away?"

He blocked her path back to the couch. "I'm not sure you can."

"Who are the girls?"

"She didn't tell you?"

Tanya shook her head, needing to know who would dare hurt her daughter.

"I don't know them. I thought this week when I go to the center to tutor I would ask around and find out."

"All she would tell me is that they are sophomores."

"Okay, that helps."

Suddenly the very act of standing erect tired her as though someone from above were pressing her down. She covered the short distance to the couch and collapsed onto it. The physical and emotional energy she had expended was catching up with her. "I promised her for the time being I wouldn't do anything. I don't know how I'm gonna keep that promise. All I want to do is find out who those girls are and have a few choice words with them and then their parents."

"You can't, at least not yet." Chance eased down next to her and took her hand. "You promised her."

"I told her I would give her a chance to work it out with them, but if she can't, I'll have to do something."

"What?"

She lifted her shoulders. "Beats me. Any suggestions?"

He sagged back. "No. This is out of my realm of expertise. When Haley had trouble with another girl, she went to her mother."

"I can't believe how mean some girls can be. What in the world has my daughter done to them? Do you think it's because she is in a wheelchair?"

His hand linked with hers, he answered, "Maybe."

"They might as well have pushed Crystal from her wheelchair this afternoon. They knew what their actions would do." Tears smarted her eyes, roughened her voice.

Chance slipped an arm around her and brought her up against his side. "I think you're right. Let me see what I can find out at the center."

Comforted by his presence, Tanya laid her head on his shoulder. "I'd wanted Crystal to get more involved at the center, but if girls like that are gonna be there, I probably shouldn't encourage her to go."

"Why don't I take her with me when I go to

tutor? She's a whiz at math. Maybe she could tutor someone, too."

"I don't know."

"I won't let anything happen to her. I'll keep an eye on her. Helping others always makes a person feel better."

Lately she had turned to Chance more and more. What was going to happen when he left? Already she felt the emptiness in her heart as she thought of that day. She had to protect herself from being hurt.

"Fine." She slid her eyes closed, a tear leaking out. She knew that Chance would do all that was humanly possible to protect Crystal, but this might be beyond him.

Lord, open those girls' eyes. Help them to see what harm they are doing to my daughter. And please guide me in how to deal with these growing feelings I have for Chance. I'm going to need You when he leaves Sweetwater.

"I've never seen two kids so excited to see someone," Jesse said as she brought the decaf coffee out onto the deck.

Above the squawking of the two geese by the lake, Tanya said, "Crystal's been thinking of doing some babysitting to earn some money."

"Great! I know Cindy and Nate would be thrilled." Jesse poured some coffee into two mugs.

"I don't know if it's a good idea. The logistics would be hard with her wheelchair. Most houses aren't easily accessible for her. Yours isn't too bad, but others are. That's why I haven't encouraged her."

"She wants to earn some money? Maybe she could do something else."

Tanya sipped her drink. "Like what?"

"Let me think on it."

The din caused by Fred and Ethel, two geese that lived at Jesse's house, increased. Tanya stretched her neck to look over the railing, the light on the pole enabling her to see Nick and Chance near the pier. "What are they doing down by the lake?"

"Nick's probably taunting Fred. He's never been a big fan of Fred's since that day he nipped him on the leg."

"Ah, but wasn't that the first time you met Nick?"

"Yep."

"He should be indebted to Fred."

Jesse arched a brow. "You would think. But he keeps telling me he would have discovered me eventually on his own."

The honking subsided as Chance and Nick

hiked back toward the house. Momentarily the two men disappeared as the dark swallowed them. When they came into the circle of light from the deck, Tanya's heart rate accelerated. For a few seconds she recalled the sensation of Chance's arm casually about her as they'd sat on his couch. She'd felt protected and cherished while he had comforted her about Crystal. She hadn't felt so alone with him next to her.

"It's about time you two came back. I was about to go and get you. Poor Fred and Ethel."

Jesse's words dragged Tanya from her daydreaming as Nick said, "There's nothing poor about either of those geese." He climbed the steps to the deck with Chance slightly behind him. "I wanted to show Chance our new pier, offer him the use of the boat if he wants to fish."

Tanya sensed Chance's eyes on her. She swung her gaze to his and became lost in the glittering blue, much like the very lake only a hundred yards away on a sunlit day. "You like to fish?"

"No. Well, I don't know. I've never gone fishing." Chance found the place on the love seat next to Tanya and folded his long length onto it. "Want to teach me?"

"Can't. I don't know how, either." Along the

side pressed against Chance's, her body tingled from the connection.

"I guess I'll have one less opponent at the fishing rodeo." Nick took a chair across from them.

"What fishing rodeo?" Chance asked, taking a mug that Jesse had filled with coffee.

"The one associated with the Last Chance Picnic next weekend. The prize for the biggest fish is a dinner for two at Andre's." A competitive gleam shone in Nick's eyes.

"Nick Blackburn, we were just there two weeks ago," Jesse said, shaking her head.

"I know. But I'm gonna beat your granddad this year. Besides, my entry fee goes toward a good cause, the youth center."

"I'm curious why it's called the Last Chance Picnic." Chance cupped his mug between his two hands.

"It's the last chance before winter." Tanya angled herself so she faced Chance on the love seat. "It's always the first weekend in November. There have been a few years we've had to go indoors because it was raining. Once it snowed. We've always used the picnic as a fund-raiser for a worthy cause. Each year the town council comes up with a new one. It's all day. Most of the residents come for at least a short time."

Snapping her fingers, Jesse said, "I've got it. I know how Crystal can make some money."

"She's looking for a job?" Chance asked then took several swallows of his coffee before placing it on the glass table in front of him.

"Yeah, like every other teen, she wants her own money." Jesse turned toward Tanya. "What if she drew a portrait of Nate and Cindy with Bingo and Oreo? Do you think she'll do it?"

"I—I—" After what happened today at the center, would her daughter associate drawing with being harassed? Had something Crystal done in art class set the girls off? Would that stop her from drawing? "I don't know."

"I hope she will. I've seen her work and she's very talented." Jesse surged to her feet. "I'd better check on the kids. Be back in a sec."

"Jesse, don't say anything to Crystal. I'll talk to her."

Jesse gave her a funny look and shrugged. "Sure."

While her friend disappeared inside the house, Tanya wondered how her daughter would react to Jesse's proposal. Like herself, Crystal had kept her ability a private affair, only sharing with a select few. Knowing Jesse, she would frame the drawing and display it for everyone to see in her living room.

The ringing of Nick's cell phone cut into the silence that followed his wife's departure. "Excuse me. I've got to take this."

"What's wrong?" Chance asked when they were left alone on the deck.

"The girls were taunting Crystal with her sketchbook. Was there something in it that set them off?"

"Maybe. And you're worried that this incident will affect Crystal's desire to draw?"

"She doesn't have a lot she can do. Drawing and singing are two things she enjoys. I don't want to see their viciousness destroying that."

He took her hand, threading his fingers through hers. "Those girls can't destroy her talent, and as far as her desire to draw, only Crystal really controls that."

"But if I know Jesse, she'll talk my daughter into doing the portrait and then publicize Crystal's 'new' business."

"What's wrong with that? She wants to make some money."

"That will give those girls more fuel to use against Crystal."

His brows slashed downward, his forehead creased. "So she should hide her talent?"

"What if they make fun of her drawings?"

"She'll deal with it and consider the source." Chance rose and pulled her toward him. "It isn't Crystal we're talking about, is it?"

His sharp gaze snared hers. Her throat went dry. She opened her mouth but no words came out. She didn't want to think about her teenage years when a group of popular girls had taunted her, chipping away at the self-confidence that she had felt when she drew people. Only lately had she begun slowly to redevelop that desire to draw others when she'd taught her daughter what she knew.

"Tanya?"

She nodded, still not able to form an answer.

He brought his hands up and clasped her head, his gaze seeming to bore into her. "I know one thing. Both mother and daughter are very talented, and nobody can take that away from you two unless you let them. You were given an ability most don't have. Share it with the world."

His words bolstered her spirits. Rationally she knew he was right. Emotionally she had scars that had barely healed. Exposing her inner self to others' eyes scared her. She'd spent her teenage years trying to belong and never quite feeling as though she did. It had taken Tom's love to bring her out of her shell, then his support had been pulled out from under her. Only God's love and her circle of friends had held her together since Tom's arrest and conviction.

Chance plowed one hand through her hair, gently prodding her forward—toward his mouth. When it settled over hers, her world tilted and spun as though she rode a dizzying ride. She clung to him, her fingers digging into his shoulders to steady her as her legs trembled.

When they finally parted, his shallow breath mingled with hers. Just a hint of coffee laced it.

He rested his forehead against hers. "You were given a talent. Celebrate that talent. Proclaim it to the world. Most people can't do what you can. Believe in yourself, Tanya."

"I'm trying."

"Look at what you've done so far," he said and leaned back to get a better glimpse of her. "You've raised a beautiful, caring daughter. You've shared your talent and knowledge with her. You're dealing with being bipolar."

The word *bipolar* from Chance's lips stunned her. He knew! Who had told him? Crystal? Tom? One of her friends?

"Tanya?" Chance's smile evolved into a frown.

She jerked away. "How did you find out?" She barely got the question past her suddenly parched lips.

"Tom."

She inhaled then exhaled—slow, deep breaths that weren't enough to fill her lungs. "I should have known. He was never comfortable with my—" she searched for the right word to use "—illness."

"He wasn't. He admitted it to me." Chance gathered her into his arms. "You amaze me. You've gone through so much and dealt with it well. You've befriended me when I needed it the most."

She was afraid it was more than befriending. How could she stop herself from falling off a mountain when she stood on the very tip, ready to plunge with the least push? The very thought wrung her heart.

"I don't know, Chance, if this is such a good idea. Most upperclassmen wouldn't want to be tutored by a freshman." Crystal powered her wheelchair up the ramp that led to the front doors of the youth center.

"Dane said there was a whole list of kids

signed up who needed help in algebra and geometry. You're a math whiz so why not share the wealth?"

Crystal shot him a skeptical glance before she went through the door he held open. Charlie trotted in after her then Chance followed. Sounds of a basketball striking the floor echoed through the hall that led from the gym. A cheer reverberated, then another.

"We've got the first classroom on the left," Chance said, stopping next to Crystal in the doorway into the gym.

A wistful look on her face underscored her longing to be a part of the group of teens playing an impromptu game while a few by-standers watched. Stroking her service dog absently, she sighed, then turned her wheel-chair toward the classroom area of the building.

Dane exited the room and smiled at them. "I've got four kids waiting. Another is coming later."

"Great. I've brought help. In fact, Crystal probably would do better than me. It's been a while since I looked at this level of math."

"It's like riding a bike, Chance. I'm sure it'll come back once you see it," Crystal said and directed her chair through the entrance into the classroom.

She came to an abrupt halt only a foot inside, causing Chance to bump into the back of her wheelchair. He peered down. The color bled from her face, Crystal's gaze riveted to a girl sitting next to Eddy O'Neal.

Chapter Seven

❦

Chance's gut clenched. One of the girls who had harassed Crystal in the TV room sat next to Eddy. The teen with long blond hair pulled back in a ponytail laughed at something Eddy said, then glanced up and caught sight of Crystal. The smile that had accompanied the girl's laughter froze, then melted into a pout.

The teenager slammed her geometry book closed and shot to her feet. Snatching up her purse, she gathered up her work and stormed toward the door. "See ya, Eddy. I think I can figure this out."

Crystal quickly maneuvered her wheelchair out of the girl's way while Chance said, "If you change your mind and decide you need help, you know where to find us."

The blonde stabbed Chance with a withering

look. "From an ex-con and—" her hard gaze slid to Crystal "—I don't think so."

Chance sidled toward Crystal, gripping the back of her wheelchair. "Your loss."

When he faced the other three teens, one girl and two boys, in the room, he hoped that his anger didn't register on his face even though inside he shook with its force. "Why don't you all tell me what you need help with?"

"Algebra II," Eddy said with a smile.

Chance was glad to see the young man who Dane had introduced him to that first day he had come to the center. "Okay. What else?" He scanned the faces of the others.

The other boy, who Chance was almost sure was the same one that Crystal had drawn over and over, said, "Algebra I."

Chance slid a glance toward Crystal, who purposefully avoided eye contact with the boy.

"Geometry." The lone girl sat off to the side away from the others.

"Okay. I'll work with you, Eddy, and…"

"Grant Foster," the other boy said.

"And Crystal will help you." Chance regarded the girl and wondered if she were a friend of the other one.

"I'm Amanda and that's great. I can use all

the help I can get. My friend will be here in a few minutes."

Still not looking at Grant, Crystal peered toward the door as though she expected the other girl to come back and dump her from her wheelchair. Chance turned his back on the group and spoke in a low tone, "If you don't want to help, I'll understand."

Crystal's eyes grew round. "No, I'll stay in here. I might as well help Amanda while I wait for you."

"I can call your mom, and she can come get you if you want."

"No, I came to help. I'm not gonna let Holly run me off." Her voice quavered with her declaration.

"Are you okay with Grant being in here?"

"Why wouldn't I be?" Crystal kept her head down.

"You're very talented, Crystal. I know he was the boy you were drawing."

She finally glanced up at him. "He needs help."

"Then let's get started."

While Chance sat across from Grant and Eddy, Crystal situated her wheelchair at the end of the table near Amanda. She gave the girl a smile that was immediately returned. The tension in Crystal's face relaxed, and Chance hoped that he hadn't been wrong in persuading her to help others with their math.

"Mr. Taylor, I'm sorry about Holly." Eddy shook his head. "I don't know what's got into her. Right before you came she was talking about the trouble she was having in geometry. I was trying to help her, but she didn't understand my explanation."

Frankly Chance didn't know what had gotten into Holly, either, but he replied, "She's the one who'll have to find the help she needs. I don't want anyone here unless he wants to be. Now show me what you're working on and what's the problem. I'll start with you Eddy, then work with you, Grant."

As Eddy opened his book and flipped to the page, Chance heard Crystal's giggle and peered at the two girls, their heads bent over the paper Crystal wrote on. *Thank You, God.* The second he thought the words, surprise flitted through him. He'd stopped praying to the Lord over two years ago.

Tanya tossed her head back and relished the warm rays of the sun as it beat down upon her. The scent of dirt, grass and trees saturated the air. The sounds of nature—water lapping against the shore, a chirping bird sitting on a nearby limb, the buzz and hum of the insects—vied with the voices of the townspeople as they arrived at the city park along the lake for the Last Chance Picnic celebration.

The event's very name made her think of the man who had distracted her more and more each day he was in her life. When she caught a glimpse of a certain sadness in his eyes, she sensed this was Chance's last chance at happiness. Knowing his background only confirmed that impression.

When Tanya plopped into a lawn chair under a large oak, she surveyed the scene before her. Food covered the park's picnic tables while huge garbage cans filled with ice held soft drinks and bottled water. She noticed Jesse still manned the booth at the entrance, taking up the fee to attend this fund-raiser for the youth center. Off to the side in the open field Chance helped Dane and Nick set up the volleyball net while Joshua and Samuel organized the young children into groups for the fun races.

"If Zoey sees you just sitting, she'll have your head," Beth said, taking the chair next to Tanya.

"How about you?"

"Mine, too. But after setting up the food the past two hours, I'm exhausted." Beth smoothed her maternity blouse down.

"Ditto. I never knew fun could be so much work."

Beth gestured toward the crowds arriving. "But what a success. I think this is the best year yet."

"It's for a good cause."

"You can say that again. Jane told me that Dane's got the tutoring program up and running. The kids are flocking to get help. She's even volunteered to help in math."

"So has Crystal."

"Yeah, I know. Jane told me she's helping several girls with their geometry."

"Two evenings last week and she's actually been upbeat about going to school for the first time in months. Amanda, one of the girls she's tutoring, called her last night to just talk. When Crystal got off the phone, she was beaming."

"I'm glad you encouraged her to get involved."

"I didn't. Chance did." When Tanya thought about it, Chance had touched many facets of hers and Crystal's lives at a time when they'd needed it. *Thank You, Lord, for sending him.* But she wanted—needed—to help him. *How, Lord? Show me.*

"Speaking of Chance, he's been quite a hit with several of the teens. I saw Eddy earlier and he was so pumped. He passed his math test yesterday. He's been spreading the word about

Chance. It seems your tenant has quite a gift with teaching."

The slight emphasis on the word *your* caused heat to creep up Tanya's neck. "Yes, he is gifted." In many ways, she added silently, thinking of his quiet presence in her life that made her cherish each moment spent with him.

"I will warn you, though, that a few parents aren't happy that Chance is tutoring at the center. It was one thing when he donated his time doing the books. But some of them are upset that he is actually working with the teenagers. They've complained to Dane and Samuel."

"What is it about being innocent that they don't understand?" Tanya asked in a loud enough voice that several people nearby glanced at her with a question on their faces. She ignored them and lowered her tone, adding, "We need to do something, Beth."

"Yeah, I was thinking the same thing. Our support should help."

"There's gotta be more we can do." Tanya searched the crowd forming near the volleyball area and found Chance in the middle with Dane on one side and Eddy on the other.

"We'll need to pray about it. Something will come to mind. I'll tell Darcy, Zoey and Jesse to pray, too."

"That's an awful lot of praying power."

"Hey, we're a force to reckon with and the townspeople spreading the rumors will soon find that out."

"I almost feel sorry for them," Tanya said with a laugh.

"Feel sorry for who?" Darcy lowered herself into the vacant chair on the other side of Beth.

"The people who won't let Chance live in peace." Tanya's eyes found Chance again. Peace. Had he experienced any of that lately? She doubted it.

"I don't feel sorry for them. They are mean-spirited and need to mind their own business." Darcy folded her hands over her protruding stomach. "Bring them on. No one should mess with a woman who's suddenly carrying an extra twenty-five pounds."

Beth raised both brows. "When's your baby due?"

"Beth Morgan, you know exactly when my baby is due. About eight weeks before yours. And yes, I've gained more weight than I wanted to."

Again Tanya couldn't resist scanning the people in the two-acre field where the activities would take place, seeking the man under discussion. She enjoyed watching him interact with others. When her gaze lit upon him, he was in the middle of his own discussion with a group of teenage boys preparing to play the first game of volleyball. Chance looked up, his eyes connecting with hers. Even from this distance she could feel the intensity in his regard. One corner of his mouth hitched up in that grin that could melt ice.

Chance's team gave a cheer, then broke their huddle and loped out onto the makeshift court. His gaze remained on her.

She'd rested enough. Rising, she said to Beth and Darcy, "Excuse me. I think I'll watch the volleyball game that's about to start."

"Hmm, I wonder why she has a sudden interest in volleyball," Darcy said as Tanya hurried toward the reason she had a sudden interest in a game she had no idea how to play.

"Hi." She came to a stop beside Chance.

"Hi, yourself. You looked mighty comfortable in that chair."

"I'm afraid if I sit too long, I'll never get up. So, can I help you with the game?"

One brow arched. "You play volleyball?"

"Well, no, but I figure it isn't too hard. Besides, I'm not offering to play, just help."

His full-fledged grin moved across his mouth. "I'm here to cheer these guys on. That's all."

"You aren't gonna play?"

He tossed his head in the direction of the grass court. "Do you see anyone out there over the age of twenty?"

She looked, then shook her head. "Then you're just coaching them?"

"No. Eddy is the team captain and very capable of coaching them. I'm their moral support."

The game started with Dane standing on the other side of the court, cheering whoever hit the ball no matter which team, while Chance supported the players with quiet words of encouragement, as though he didn't want to call attention to himself. She followed the action for a few minutes, but she couldn't shake the feeling that something was going on with Chance. The activities for the kids were off to the side away from most of the people who attended the picnic.

Finally when one side rotated, causing a lull in the game, Tanya asked, "You've been over here most of the morning. Is something wrong?"

Again one of his brows quirked as he assessed her. "I gather you've heard about the complaints against me tutoring at the youth center."

"Yep. Do you know who is complaining?"

"Dane and Samuel didn't feel they could say,

but I've got a pretty good idea, starting with Holly Proctor's parents."

"Holly? The family used to go to our church. They stopped attending a few years back. Why do you think they complained?" A finely honed tension straightened her spine.

"She wasn't too happy the other evening when Crystal and I showed up to tutor. She left in a huff."

"Well, she can be dramatic at times."

"There's more. She was one of the girls who harassed Crystal in the TV room at the center."

A surge of anger zipped through Tanya. "And you're just now telling me this?"

"Yes, we've both been busy this week."

She glared at him. "Chance Taylor, you didn't think that bit of information warranted a visit even in the midst of your busy schedule?"

"Okay, I was hoping that Crystal would tell you. Obviously she didn't."

"Probably because she knows I will have a hard time not saying something to at least Holly's parents."

"See, I was trying to help you keep your promise to your daughter."

"You know there wasn't a timeline established on how long I would let her try to solve this problem."

Her gaze swept the crowd of people milling around and located the Proctor family with Holly standing off to the side slightly, a pout on her face, her arms crossed. One of the teenager's friends approached Holly and her sullen expression transformed into less grim lines. They further separated themselves from Holly's parents, whispering and glancing around them. Crystal's tormentor laughed when a younger girl walked by.

The urge to shake some sense into the teenager flooded Tanya. She started toward the pair. Chance's hand on her arm stopped her. She stared down at the long fingers clasped around her, then up into his eyes, so full of concern. "Someone needs to straighten Holly out. She shouldn't treat people like that."

"True. But I have a feeling that Crystal wouldn't like you interfering. Remember what you said to her last weekend."

"I'm supposed to do *nothing?*" Her nails dug into her palms.

"You can support Crystal. Be there to listen."

"Then how about you? You aren't gonna let those few parents stop you from tutoring, are you?"

His face tensed. "No. As long as there are kids to tutor and Dane allows me to, I will."

A cheer erupted behind Tanya. She glanced over her shoulder at the volleyball court and saw several teenagers leap into the air. Eddy came down, slamming the ball over the net. A boy on the other team dived for it and missed. The high-fives and shouts of victory drew a good part of the townspeople's attention toward them.

As Chance congratulated the winners, Tanya glimpsed Jim Proctor catch sight of Chance and frown, then say something to his wife. He strode toward Dane, still on the other side of the court with Samuel, who had joined him a few minutes ago. The man's path took him by Wilbur Thompson and Felicia Winters. Jim solicited their assistance and en masse they cornered Dane and Samuel with several other adults strolling toward the gathering.

Chance grew quiet, his gaze on the group quickly forming across the volleyball court. He flinched at the sound of a raised voice and turned away.

"I'll be right back," Tanya muttered and stalked toward the group, half expecting Chance to stop her. But the fact he didn't alarmed her more than if he had tried. The hurt expression on his face before he'd masked it behind a bland one stiffened her resolve. He was a good man and it was about time the people of Sweetwater knew that!

"But he's been in prison," Wilbur said, glaring at Dane. "I don't want my grandchildren around someone like him."

"Then don't let them come to the center." Dane returned Wilbur's glare.

Spying Zoey and Beth making a beeline toward the group, Tanya pushed her way through the crowd until she stood next to Dane and Samuel.

"The people volunteering at the center should be checked out. My son should do a thorough background check on them." Wilbur pounded his fist into his palm.

Behind the older man, Zach Thompson, the town's police chief said, "Dad, I have and Chance checks out."

Wilbur huffed while Jim shouldered his way to the center of the circle of townspeople. "My daughter can't even get the help she needs because she's afraid."

Words of anger gushed upward, and Tanya had to bite them back. She'd promised her daughter she wouldn't say anything about Holly's actions—at least not yet. But as far as Tanya was concerned, there was probably little that frightened that young woman. Instead, Holly was the cause of scaring others.

Zoey came forward. "We have a list of tutors

she can access through the counseling office. If you want some names, Jim, you can call me on Monday morning."

"Those tutors cost money."

"I'll help her."

The sound of her daughter's voice sent a shock wave through Tanya. She spun around and faced Crystal, who had maneuvered her wheelchair between the adults. Amanda walked beside her.

"For free. But she'll have to come to my house or the center if she wants help." Crystal stopped next to Tanya.

Jim opened and closed his mouth, then finally said, "*He* lives next to you."

Tanya placed her hand on her daughter's shoulder for a few seconds, then stepped forward until she invaded the man's personal space. Anger vibrated through her, but she instilled an even level into her voice as she said, "And he's a good neighbor. He doesn't judge. He helps others when he sees a need. I couldn't ask for a better neighbor. So if you want *free* tutoring, you have a choice. Take up my daughter's offer and come to the house or go to the center."

For half a minute Jim glared at her, then looked toward Zoey. "Send the list home with

Holly on Monday. I refuse to expose my daughter to a man like that." Then he plunged into the crowd, disappearing from Tanya's view.

"I don't know about you, but I'm starved. I suggest we remember why we have this Last Chance Picnic and proceed to the tables set up with the food." Samuel's sharp gaze slid from one irate adult to the next, staring down each one until he hurried away.

After the instigators left, Beth said, "I've never been so embarrassed by our neighbors' behavior as today. Where in the world is this coming from?"

"It only takes a few to stir up the others." Dane clasped Zoey's hand and pulled her against his side.

"You mean Wilbur." Tanya positioned herself next to her daughter, her hand on her shoulder again. She was so proud of Crystal for offering to help the one person who was the cause of her agony.

"Yeah. Remember the problems I had with him when *I* first came to town? He just doesn't know how to keep his nose out of other people's business." Dane scanned the area. "Where's Chance?"

Tanya shifted until she made her own survey

of the park. Chance wasn't anywhere to be seen, not even with Nick and Jesse or Eddy and his friends. Alarm bubbled up. *He's left. And I can't blame him. Will this push him to leave Sweetwater?* The question intensified the alarm, her stomach constricting.

Then she caught sight of him on the other side of the park near the water. When the police chief approached him, Chance stiffened. Even from this distance Tanya saw the wariness in every line of Chance's body.

"I see him. I'll be back." Tanya avoided the groups of townspeople and rushed across the expanse of the park toward him.

As she neared him, Chance shook Zach's hand, saying something to the police chief that was too low for her to hear. But when Zach left and passed her, he nodded, his features relaxed in a grin.

Although Chance saw her approach, he faced the lake, his hands stuffed into the front pockets of his jeans. The breeze from the water played with his hair, which he'd let grow out since his arrival in Sweetwater. Tanya slowed her pace, taking in his hunched shoulders, his rigid stance, as though a cold wind battered his body.

"I'm sorry you had to witness that little scene, Chance."

He didn't say anything for a long moment,

then he turned slightly. Even though his tension slipped from his expression, it still gripped his posture. "You have nothing to apologize for. This isn't the first time and I doubt it will be the last, either." He stared again at the water lapping against the shore near his feet, just missing soaking his tennis shoes.

She sidled up next to him, her gaze trained on a couple of skiffs on the lake a few hundred yards out, their occupants participating in the fishing rodeo. "What did Zach have to say?" Although she had intended for her voice to be casual, she winced at the intensity in the question.

"About the same as you, except he was more specific. He was apologizing for his father's rude behavior."

"He shouldn't apologize. Wilbur should."

"That's not gonna happen. Wilbur thinks he's protecting the people of this good town."

Tanya snorted. "From you? Wilbur is a busybody who needs to mind his own business." Even though his body language screamed stay away, Tanya slipped her arm through his. "And Jim Proctor needs to take care of his own problems. His daughter is a menace."

He chuckled, relaxing some more. "Remind me not to get on your bad side. You're fierce when riled." He twisted toward her, so near his clean scent laced the air between them and mingled with the more earthy odors surrounding them. "But I don't need you to fight my battles."

"First Crystal and now you. Will no one let me help them?"

"The best way to deal with the Wilburs and Jims of this world is to ignore them and prove them wrong by doing the best job you can."

She caressed his face, feeling the slightly rough texture of his jawline. "But you aren't ignoring them really. I saw the look of hurt in your eyes."

Those eyes crinkled with humor now. "I didn't say I had mastered the best way yet. I'm still working on it." He searched her features, as though seeking some answers to questions she didn't know. "Let's go for a walk."

She fit her hand within his, and they started along the path that followed the shoreline. The aroma of grilled hamburgers floated to her, and she realized some of the men were cooking lunch. Even though hunger pangs tightened her stomach, she wouldn't be any other place but beside Chance. Maybe this would be the time he would let her inside, and she would be able to help him.

The large oaks, maples and pines that lined

the trail shielded them from the sun, but an occasional ray fought its way through the multicolored canopy of fall leaves and struck the dirt path with its brightness. The coolness of the forest cloaked Tanya as she waited for Chance to break the silence.

"What did Crystal say about doing a portrait of Nate and Cindy?"

"I haven't said anything to her about Jesse's offer."

He slanted a look at her. "Why not?"

"Because…because…" Tanya couldn't get the words past her lips. Wasn't it obvious she was protecting her daughter?

"Tanya, what's going on? Crystal would do an excellent job."

"I'm sure she would."

"Then why haven't you told her?"

She swallowed several times. "Because it could open her up to more ridicule. She's got enough to deal with at the moment."

He stopped, angling toward her and clasping her arms. "What happened to you to make you hide your talent?"

"I made the mistake of entering an art contest at school and winning against a girl who was very popular and had many friends. She wasn't a gracious loser. She made my life a living nightmare for the rest of the year until we moved here to Sweetwater."

"And so you stopped drawing."

"I drew. Just no one saw my drawings after that. Look what happened when Holly saw Crystal at the art lesson at the center. Can you imagine what that girl would do if Crystal starting earning money with her art?"

He rested his forehead against hers. "Yes, I can imagine. But shouldn't Crystal make up her own mind what she needs to do? She wants to earn some money and that would be a good way for her to do something with her talent."

Tanya thought back to Crystal in the middle of the crowd earlier, telling Jim Proctor she would tutor his daughter for free. In her mind's eye she pictured the lift of her daughter's chin, the determination in her eyes and knew that Crystal meant every word she had uttered. She was turning the other cheek so to speak, doing what Christ would want her to do.

"I'll tell her this evening. It'll be her choice."

Chance brushed her hair behind her ears, his gaze riveted to hers. Her mouth went dry, her heartbeat pounding in her ears and drowning out all sounds. All her senses focused on him only inches from her, a tingling awareness blanketing her.

He leaned in and feathered his lips over hers. They reacted by parting. His mouth came down on hers possessing it as though there were no tomorrows. His arms entwined about her and pressed her against him while she surrendered to his kiss.

A good minute later he raised his head, the tight band of his embrace loosening slightly. A corner of his mouth lifted, his cheeks dimpling.

She brushed her finger over each indentation. "You know this was supposed to be a conversation about you and somehow we ended up discussing me. Chance Taylor, you're quite good at changing the subject."

"I'm glad I'm good at something."

"Oh, there are a number of things you are good at," she said, reliving the kiss he had just given her.

Chapter Eight

Tanya opened the drawer in the bathroom and found her medications for manic depression. She'd been feeling so well lately. In spite of all that had happened the past year, she'd done well mentally. Maybe she didn't have to take her two medicines anymore.

Fingering one of the bottles, she remembered the past few weeks since the Last Chance Picnic. Crystal seemed happier, especially with her and Amanda becoming closer as friends. She didn't think there had been another incident with those girls harassing her.

Thank You, Lord, for that.

Contentment shimmied down Tanya's length. She picked up the bottle, rolling it between her hands, the plastic container cool in her palms. Then there was Chance. Even though the weather had turned nasty, becoming colder than usual for this time of year, they jogged almost every evening after work along the lighted streets in the neighborhood. They often shared a dinner or two each week after he and Crystal tutored at the center. That was the least she could do since he was watching out for her daughter while there.

She stared at the white bottle. She hated depending on the pills to keep her even keel. The past three weeks had been near perfect. Maybe she could try not taking them today and see what would happen. If she could stop taking her medications for manic depression, then everything would really be perfect.

She tossed up the plastic container and snatched it from the air, the temptation growing within her. To be free, not sick, would be wonderful. To be whole for Chance.

"Mom, Chance is here."

Her daughter's shout penetrated the small bathroom. Sighing, she twisted the cap and shook a pill into her palm. Then she picked up the other bottle and removed her correct dose. She closed her fist around the medication. Better not take a chance with it being Thanksgiving. But perhaps she could speak with her doctor about it.

"Mom!"

"Coming." Tanya popped both pills into her mouth and swallowed some water, then opened the door. "With all your shouting you'd think it was a holiday or something."

"Funny, Mom. I'm starved. How long till dinner?"

With the house infused with the smells of the holiday, Tanya checked her watch. "About an hour. Why don't you set the dining room table and I'll finish up in the kitchen?"

Crystal made a one-eighty turn and headed down the hall. Her child's grin, which was appearing more and more, made Tanya cherish the moments. The aroma of the baking turkey finally prodded her into action. She still had to do a few things in order for dinner to be completed in an hour. Hurrying after her daughter, she started across the living room only to come to a halt with the sight of Chance kneeling in front of the fireplace as he lit the logs.

He looked at home in her house. She squeezed her eyes closed for a moment, needing to erase that image from her mind but unable to. When she peered at him again, his gaze pinned her with an intensity that stole her breath. He slowly rose and walked toward her. Her heart increased its beat, leaving her defenseless to his charm.

He clasped her upper arm and drew her to him. "You look beautiful."

She felt beautiful in his eyes. "You're not too bad yourself."

He cupped the back of her head, angling her so his lips caressed hers ever so lightly. "Happy Thanksgiving."

Hearing the sound of Crystal's wheelchair parted them. Tanya's heart still beat so rapidly her breaths came out in pants until she forced deep gulps of air into her oxygen-deprived lungs.

"We never build a fire, Chance. Thanks." Crystal sat in the entrance from the dining room with the dinner plates on her lap and her service dog next to her. "It's been so cold lately. This is perfect."

"Yeah, whatever happened to fall? We went from summer to winter in two weeks." Tanya continued her trek toward the kitchen, having enjoyed her little diversion in the living room.

At the oven she opened the door, heat blasting her in the face, and moved the large baking pan over to put in the dressing. As she made the tossed green salad, dicing the tomatoes, carrots and avocados, the added aroma of the dressing with its corn bread, onions, celery and mushrooms, filled every corner of the room.

"Can I help? Crystal says she doesn't need any and sent me in here."

Chance's deep voice flowed over Tanya, reminding her of that brief moment in the living room. He hadn't really kissed her, but her reaction had been as strong as if he had. Actually a mere look or touch could do that to her.

I'm falling in love with him.

That realization caused her to drop her knife before she cut herself. Her hands trembled with the knowledge of how important Chance had become to her in two months. She awoke each day looking forward to seeing him, perhaps sharing some time with him.

"Tanya?"

He stood behind her, her body reacting to his nearness—her mouth going dry, her palms damp, her pulse racing. *Get a grip. He can't ever know. It would send him fleeing from Sweetwater as fast as the next bus could take him. He's made it clear a relationship is the last thing he wants in his life right now.*

Plastering a smile on her face, she swung around to face him and wished she could step back, but the counter trapped her close to him. "You're our guest. I've got everything under control. *Everything except myself,*" she added silently.

"It smells wonderful." He moved to the side and leaned against the counter next to where she was working.

Not far enough away. But she resumed slicing the cherry tomatoes in half and putting them in the large wooden bowl. His slightest movement registered on her brain. In light of what she'd discovered about her feelings toward him, she wasn't surprised.

"Do you have to work tomorrow?"

She nodded. "Why?"

"I thought if you didn't go to work we could run in the morning since it's so cold, especially in the evening after dark."

"Sorry. It *would* be nice to run in daylight for a change. If you want to jog in the morning, go ahead. I'll understand."

"No, I can wait until you get home. I could always get started on my holiday shopping."

"Like every other person in Sweetwater."

"On second thought, I'll hold off. I don't like crowds."

She slanted a look toward him, seeing more than she suspected he wanted to show. Crowds meant people like Wilbur Thompson and Jim Proctor. She couldn't blame him for wanting to avoid them. Although they had been quiet lately because of her circle of friends and their husbands' fierce advocacy of Chance, she was sure that wouldn't remain the case. Those two liked to cause trouble. "You might be out of luck. From here until Christmas there will be crowds."

"But nothing like the day after Thanksgiving."

"Will you be okay with the Christmas lights ceremony this evening? There will be lots of people attending."

His smile didn't reach his eyes. "But it'll be dark."

"We could go late and stand in the back."

"No, Crystal will miss some of the ceremony since she'll be sitting. We'll go early and be in the front."

"Are you sure?"

"Yeah." He pushed away from the counter. "I could always go into work tomorrow. There's plenty for me to do even though Nick has closed the office."

"Ah, working during a holiday. Better watch out. You may find yourself doing more of that." Tanya chopped up a cucumber. The sound of the knife hitting the wooden board echoed in the sudden silence. She peered toward Chance.

His face was pinched into a frown, his eyes fierce. "No, never again."

The strength behind his words took her by surprise. She scooped up the pieces of cucumber and dropped them into the salad bowl, forcing a lightness into her voice. "Why do you say that?"

"Because there was a time once when my job consumed my life to the exclusion of my family. I missed out on so much. I promised myself I would never fall into that kind of trap again. I will quit a job before I will allow that to happen."

"Is that why you aren't working as a financial advisor anymore?"

"Partly."

"What's the other reason?"

He moved away from her, his back to her. The stiffness of his shoulders meant she was treading in unwelcome territory. She waited to see if he would answer. One minute ticked into two.

"I don't think people would trust someone to advise them in financial situations when they discover I've been in prison."

"Nonsense! I mean, you're innocent." She spoke to his back as he crossed the room. "How long are you gonna let others dictate how you look at yourself? You aren't an ex-con, not really."

He spun around. "Yes, I am. I've come to accept that."

"Have you?"

"It left its mark on me whether I was innocent or not. I can't wipe those years away, no matter how much I would like to."

Tanya walked to the refrigerator and placed the salad inside, then shut the door and faced him, her hands planted on her waist. "Did Tom ever talk about Crystal and me?"

Chance blinked, surprise registering before he schooled his features into a neutral expression. "Where did that question come from?"

"I've been wondering for weeks, but since we don't talk about you being in prison, I didn't want to ask. Now we are talking about the time you spent in prison…with Tom. Did he?"

Glancing away, he heaved a sigh. "All the time."

"He did? But he wouldn't see us. He divorced me." Although she tried to keep the hurt from her voice, she heard it.

"That was the hardest thing he ever did. After your last visit when he told me about it, he had tears in his eyes."

"Then why did he do it? I know he didn't want his daughter to see him like that, but he would have gotten out eventually. Didn't he want us in his life?"

"I don't think he thought he would get out. I'll never forget the hopelessness on his face that night when we talked. Prison has a way of killing hope. It was dead in Tom."

Tanya pressed herself back against the refrigerator, her legs weak. She clutched its edge to hold herself upright. "I could have helped him. I could have reminded him that God was with—"

"Don't give me that. God isn't in prison, no matter how much Samuel wants to believe He is. He may be other places, but not there."

Tanya gasped at his harsh tone. "He *is* everywhere, even prison." Her limbs trembling, she covered the space between them. "God doesn't give up on people. People give up on Him. Give Him a second chance. Open your heart and let Him in again." She laid her hand over his chest and felt the thumping of his heart. "We have so much to be thankful for. Come to church this Sunday with Crystal and me. We have a special service where we offer our thanks to the Lord for the past year. You're free. That's something to celebrate."

He gripped her hand touching him. "I can't—"

"Please."

He slid his fingers over the back of her hand to link with hers, searching her features for some kind of answer. "I'll think about it."

"If you want a ride, I leave on Sunday at nine o'clock."

When he didn't say anything, Tanya tightened her hold on his hand and in order to fill the silence asked, "I expect you to pull into the driveway any day with a car. Wasn't that on your list of items to buy?"

"I have something else I'm saving my money for first, then I'll get a used car."

"With winter coming, walking everywhere will be harder. If I can give you a lift, just ask."

"Thankfully Sweetwater isn't so big that I can't usually get where I need to go in a short amount of time. Besides, I like to walk."

Finally she slipped her hand from his and immediately missed the physical contact. "Well, at least you're doing your bit for the environment. We probably all should walk more." Tanya checked to see how the peas were simmering, then removed the turkey from the oven and stuck in the biscuits. "Did I tell you I finally got up the nerve to apply for a better-paying job at the bank?"

"No. What?"

"A loan officer."

"When will you find out?"

"Tomorrow."

"Then you might have something to celebrate tomorrow night."

She shrugged as she withdrew a pan to make the gravy in. "I know of several other women who applied that are very qualified."

"But so are you and you're dedicated to your job."

The heat scored her cheeks, and it had nothing to do with the steam rising from the turkey pan that was several feet away on the counter. Using the pan juices, Tanya mixed the ingredients for the gravy in the pot and stirred it while it simmered, the whole time aware of Chance's presence in the kitchen.

He made himself busy by giving Crystal some assistance in getting the table set, even though she had insisted she could manage by herself. He took the salt and pepper shakers, container of real butter, the salad dressing bottles and the salad into the dining room.

We work well together—Crystal, Chance and myself. That thought fueled her overactive imagination, and she immediately pictured them as a family, sharing more than a Thanksgiving dinner.

"When am I going to get to see that portrait of Nate and Cindy you drew?" Chance followed Crystal back into the kitchen, Charlie walking beside him.

"Jesse is stopping by this evening before the lighting ceremony to pick it up. I guess it's done," her daughter said.

"It's hard sometimes to let something you've created go." Chance took his place again at the counter not far from Tanya, leaning against it casually while facing Crystal and her Lab in the center of the room.

"Yeah, what if she doesn't like it?"

"I don't think you have to worry about that," Tanya said, switching off the burners and the oven.

Crystal sighed. "I know Jesse would never say anything about not liking it. She'll like it because I'm your daughter. But I want her to *really* like it because it is good."

"You want someone to tell you the truth." All casualness drained from Chance as he straightened, picking up the platter that the turkey was on. "Go get it and I'll tell you the truth—or at least my real opinion. I will always tell you the truth."

Tanya bit down on her lower lip, the quiet heavy after her daughter's exit.

Chance stepped into the dining room and placed the platter on the table then came back into the kitchen. "I know it's good, Tanya, but I meant it when I said I would tell her the truth. Nothing good comes from lies, not even little white lies."

The sound of Crystal's approach silenced Tanya's response. The serious expression on her daughter's face tautened her nerves. Her breath lodged in her throat as she waited for Crystal to show them the picture. When she lifted it from her lap to unveil the portrait, tears misted Tanya's eyes.

The pen-and-ink drawing revealed a young boy kneeling in the grass holding his dog while a younger girl stood beside him cradling her cat to her chest. The expressions of joy on the children's faces made a person seeing the portrait smile. Her daughter's talent was amazing.

Chance studied it for a good minute.

"Well?" Crystal fidgeted in her wheelchair.

"You know, I am at a loss for words." He plowed his hand through his hair.

"Good or bad ones?"

The grin that encompassed his whole face said it all. "It's beautiful. Great. Wonderful. Stupendous." He swung his attention to Tanya. "Help me here. I'm running out of synonyms for an absolutely stunning piece of art."

"Oh, I think she's got the picture." Tanya gestured toward the beaming expression on her daughter's face.

"You really like it."

"No."

Crystal blinked, her smile fading.

"I *love* it! And if Jesse Blackburn doesn't, then something is definitely wrong with her."

Crystal blew out a rush of air. "I think I'll be able to eat now. I'm starving, but my stomach has been tied up in knots, thinking about her coming to pick it up."

"Speaking of eating, let's get the rest of the food on the table. I didn't have breakfast, and I'm starved, too," Chance said.

As if they were a true family, all three worked to put the meal on the table, then sat down and held hands while Crystal said a prayer of thanksgiving.

On the ride to Main Street where the Holiday Lights Ceremony would take place, Chance thought back over the afternoon with Tanya and Crystal. A warmth suffused him that scared him. Even the prayer that Crystal had said before the meal hadn't bothered him—it had actually soothed him. Memories of the times he, Ruth and Haley had done that very thing before eating had inundated him and hadn't sent panic through him.

What was happening to him? He didn't want to forget his wife and daughter, and yet he had found himself not thinking about them every day. Instead, he'd wondered what Tanya or Crystal was doing. He'd look forward to seeing Tanya and her bright smile of greeting when he came home. She usually managed to be around either outside or at the window if it wasn't one of their days to run or the occasional times she had to work late at the bank. And if she wasn't at the window or outside, he'd come up with a reason to knock on her back door and see how her day had gone.

He needed to leave soon—before he became so involved in their lives he couldn't. And Tanya didn't need someone like him in her life permanently. He was emotionally damaged and with her manic depression she had enough to deal with herself.

He'd been reading about manic depression and admired her even more for being able to pull her life together as she had. It hadn't been easy and would always be something she would have to deal with. He was still amazed to discover people like Abraham Lincoln and Winston Churchill had been bipolar. Look what they had accomplished!

Tanya parked behind Alice's Café, and he hopped out to man the lift for Crystal. A cold breeze shivered down his length. He needed to buy a heavier coat for the winter. He hated to spend the money when he almost had saved enough for Crystal's sports wheelchair. Although there was only one other youth in a wheelchair who expressed an interest in playing basketball, Chance knew there were several adults in Sweetwater who wanted to try forming a team. If not here in town, Lexington wasn't too far away. He wanted Crystal to have the option of playing on a team if she wanted to. It would be the perfect Christmas gift, especially since he would be leaving town right after the new year. He wanted to give Crystal and Tanya something meaningful and lasting.

He just hadn't thought of the perfect gift for Tanya yet.

"Hey, Chance, are you going to stand around staring into space all evening? We'll get lousy seats," Crystal said as she drove her wheelchair around the corner of the building that housed Alice's Café.

"It's good to hear her eager to do something again." Tanya slipped her arm through his and snuggled closer.

"Jesse had a lot to do with her good mood. As I predicted, she loved the drawing."

"Don't sell yourself short. She laughed all the way through dinner today and that's because of you."

Her compliment warmed him in the cold. "It's really not any of that. It's Amanda. They are inseparable at the center."

Walking beside him, Tanya took the same path as her daughter around the building. "And on the phone in the evening. Sean and Craig complain they never talk to Crystal like they used to. Hopefully this thing with Holly is over."

Chance chilled suddenly, all the warmth gone. "Don't count on it, Tanya. Bullies don't just go away like that." He snapped his fingers.

"I can hope, can't I?"

"Sure, but don't let that keep you from seeing what's going on." *How can I leave until the problem with Holly is taken care of? And yet, the trial is the first full week in January. I've got to be there to see justice done.*

He and Tanya emerged onto Main Street, and immediately he saw Crystal near the stage with Amanda next to her. Another girl he'd seen around the center occasionally with them joined the pair. Then two boys, one being Grant Foster, came up and stood with them. Laughter sounded as Tanya and he approached.

"Maybe we should leave them to their own devices." Seeing Crystal happy caused that same emotion in him. For so long he'd forgotten what happiness meant—until he'd come to Sweetwater, until he'd met Tanya.

"Are you suggesting we would put a damper on my daughter's fun?"

He nodded. "We're over thirty. That's a given."

"You don't believe that, do you?"

He chuckled. "No. I just want to have you to myself." Where in the world did those words come from, he thought, shocked by them as much as Tanya obviously was if her wide eyes and open mouth were any indication.

She cuddled next to him, his arm slung over her shoulder. Shortly, Jesse and Nick joined them, then Darcy and Joshua. Before long Samuel, Beth, Zoey and Dane completed the group. Surrounded by Tanya's friends—no, his, too, he had to acknowledge—he realized he had a lot to be thankful for this Thanksgiving.

He leaned down close to Tanya's ear and whispered, "I'll go to church with you and Crystal this Sunday, that is, if the invitation is still open." He added the last part in a teasing tone just so he could see her expression light up before she playfully jabbed him in the side.

"Funny. You know the invitation is a standing one."

The mayor of Sweetwater came to the mike and began the ceremony with a speech. Chance tuned out the man and scanned the crowd gathered. He spied Wilbur glaring at him with Jim and his family not far from the older man. Jim Proctor refused to look toward him as though to do so would acknowledge that he was alive and part of the town.

Chance noticed one of Holly's friends pull her away and Crystal's tormentor joined a group of teenage girls, some he had seen at the center. What he had seen he hadn't cared for. They had often been cruel and callous toward others. They had always made sure they were together in a group because it gave them a sense of power. He'd seen that in prison and he'd seen what could happen. Tom's death was a result of one of those bullying gangs.

He shuddered.

"Cold?"

Tanya's question thankfully drew him away from his past. "Are you kidding? It must be twenty."

She wound her arm around his waist. "I wouldn't be surprised if it snowed before the weekend is over. I can smell it in the air."

"All I smell is wood burning. I could use a hot cup of coffee."

"Will hot apple cider do?" Tanya whispered,

close enough that the familiar scent of lilacs rivaled the aroma of burning wood.

"Sure. Hot is the operative word."

"Good. Alice invited some of us to the café after the ceremony."

"How long does it take to throw a light switch?" Chance asked as the mayor concluded his speech about the upcoming holiday season.

"Let's see, we'll sing a few songs, then the mayor's wife will turn the lights on."

"How many songs?"

"Six, maybe seven."

"That's not a few!"

As the crowd launched into "Joy to the World," Tanya murmured close to Chance's ear, "It used to be twelve—one song for each of the twelve days of Christmas. And we ended with that one."

"Then I should count my blessings?"

"Always."

In the soft glow of the streetlight, Chance became transfixed by the intensity in Tanya's gaze. He didn't hear one word of the second or third song. His attention fixed upon the woman at his side. He savored her beauty that was on the inside as well as the outside.

Finally he joined in with the others and sang the last song, "Silent Night." As the last chord rang out in the square, the mayor's wife flipped on the lights and a brilliance filled the whole length of Main Street and the park in the middle where a massive twenty-foot Christmas tree shone with hundreds of tiny twinkling clear lights.

"The power company must be ecstatic right about now." Chance took in the whole park, lights in almost every tree, lights running along the fence that separated the children's playground from the rest of the area.

"We do tend to go all out. I figure an astronaut can see Sweetwater from outer space. What do you think?"

"Yep. I figure you're right." He hugged her against his length, enjoying her warmth, her own radiance that vied with the brilliance of the lights.

Tanya's becoming too important to me. He needed to back off. And he would tomorrow, he told himself as the crowd began to disperse, people strolling toward their parked vehicles. Some of them made their way toward Alice's Café, lit with its own bright lights, the owner standing in the doorway greeting her guests as they entered.

Tanya started for the restaurant, stopped after a few feet and said, "I forgot I have a present for Darcy. I left it in the van. I'll be right back."

Before she could move away, Chance captured her hand and halted her progress. "I'll get it. You go on inside."

She tossed him the keys, and he snatched them up. Then in a lope he headed toward the back of the building and the few parking spaces behind it. Coming around the corner, he stopped when he heard yelling.

"Can't you do anything right?" Jim stood only inches from Holly, his face thrust in hers, his hands balled into fists. "You don't need a tutor to learn math. You just need to study harder. When were you going to tell me you failed that test? If your teacher hadn't said anything tonight, I wouldn't have found out, would I?"

"Dad—"

Jim glimpsed Chance and stepped back. "Get in. We'll talk more at home."

Chance watched Holly jerk open the back door and slide inside while her mother and younger brother got into the car. Silhouetted in the dim light from the cars passing on the side street, Jim Proctor stared at Chance. The man's anger was evident by the stiff lines of his body.

So much for the perfect family, Chance thought as the Proctors pulled away, Jim gunning the car. Bullies were made and Holly had been expertly molded by her father. But still that didn't excuse the teenager's actions toward Crystal.

Quickly Chance retrieved the wrapped present for Darcy and jogged back to the front of Alice's Café. He wanted to feel sorry for Holly, but Crystal's pain made it hard for him.

When he entered the restaurant, he searched for Tanya and found her with Darcy and Joshua in the corner. Chance wove his way through the crowded café and joined them, giving the present to Tanya who immediately handed it to Darcy.

"I saw this yesterday and couldn't resist, especially since we know you're having a little girl."

Darcy took the gift. "You shouldn't have. You've already given me something."

"Yes, I should have. Darcy, you were the first person to reach out and help me when I was in trouble. I'll never forget that."

"We've helped each other." Darcy's eyes filled with tears. "See, you're gonna make me cry. I cry at the drop of a hat lately."

"Tell me about it," Joshua said with a laugh.

Darcy jabbed her husband in the side. "Are you complaining?"

He held up his hands. "No way am I answering that question."

"Unwrap the present." Tanya shifted from one foot to the other.

Darcy ripped into the gift. When she opened it to reveal a music box with painted pink roses on it, a tear slid down her face. "Oh, Tanya. It's beautiful. What song does it play?"

"That's the best part—'Amazing Grace.'"

"The one Sean and Crystal sang together."

Tanya nodded. She turned to Chance. "That was the first time they sang together and they got a standing ovation."

"It's one of my favorites," Darcy murmured, running her finger along the edge of the music box. "Thank you, Tanya. I will treasure this."

A few seconds of silence reigned before Joshua cleared his throat and said, "Hey, I don't know about you all, but I'm gonna fight my way to the counter and get some hot apple cider and a few of Alice's cookies."

"I'll help you." Chance followed Joshua, leaving the women by themselves.

"Call me tomorrow whether you get the job or not. I want to know either way." Darcy tossed the crumpled wrapping paper and box into the trash can near the kitchen door.

"I'll have more responsibility. If I get it, I'll need to go to a seminar in Lexington for three days in a couple of weeks. I'll have to drive back and forth since I can't stay overnight because of Crystal."

"She can come out to the farm and stay with us."

"No, I'd rather drive. It's only a little over an hour. I can do it for three days. With all that's happened this year at school, I don't want to be gone."

"I don't blame you, but you know we're here to help if you need it." Darcy cradled the music box to her chest. "Sean says things are a little better at school."

"The situation has improved some, especially since Crystal's begun to tutor some of the kids at the center. I think they appreciate the help."

"A bully feeds on the reactions of bystanders and if there are no bystanders…" Darcy's voice trailed off into silence as she shrugged. She looked toward Chance and Joshua who were making their way back and asked, "How's it going with Chance?"

"Fine."

"Fine? That's all you're gonna say. I saw you two at the ceremony looking all cozy. I want details."

"There are no details. We're good friends. That's all." Tanya noticed the men stopped to say something to Dane.

"That's all? That's not the way it looked to me."

"Darcy, I don't know that Chance will ever

get over his family's deaths. Not only does he have a picture of his daughter up in his apartment but one of his wife, too. I know they are together but still…"

"You need to give him a drawing of you and Crystal so he has something besides them. Life is for the living. He needs to move on and you need to help him do that."

"It's not that simple."

"Sure it is. Wouldn't that be a great Christmas gift for him? A portrait of you and Crystal. I bet he would treasure it like I will this." Darcy held up the music box. "You're not asking him to get rid of the photo of his wife and daughter. You're just giving him an alternative."

"I don't do drawings for other—"

"Shh. Here they come. Think about it." Darcy plastered a smile on her face and directed it at Joshua and Chance who broke through the crowd with their drinks in their hands.

Tanya took the mug Chance handed her and sipped the apple cider, relishing its spicy flavor. Its heat slid down her throat warming her insides.

When Chance bent forward and whispered, "I discovered something about the Proctor family that I want to share with you," the warmth from his nearness replaced the warmth from her drink.

She nearly melted into him. "What?"

"I'll tell you later, but it explains some things."

Her curiosity aroused, Tanya hardly listened to the conversation flowing around her, even when Samuel and Beth joined them. But the mention of the Proctor family caused her to scan the café to make sure her daughter was all right. Crystal sat in her wheelchair at a table with Jane, Eddy, Craig, Grant and Amanda. The grin on her daughter's face eased any tension the Proctor name produced. And it didn't return until her friend got up on a chair and gave a loud whistle to get everyone's attention.

Jesse held up the drawing Crystal did of Nate and Cindy so the crowd could see. Murmurs flew around the cafe. The noise level rose.

"I wanted you all to see what a beautiful job Crystal Bolton did on a drawing of my children that I commissioned. From what I understand she wants to earn some money and what better way than sharing her talent with us." Jesse gestured toward Crystal, who blushed from head to toe.

But a huge grin still graced her daughter's face as several people openly commented on the portrait. Two women approached her immediately and Tanya could see her pleasure at their compliments.

"Her work was shown and nothing bad

happened. Crystal is doing a great job of handling the praise. I predict she will have to turn people down before the evening is over. She's gonna be quite busy this holiday season. Maybe you could help her out with some of the portraits?"

Chance's suggestion stirred Tanya's interest for all of two seconds until she pictured people staring at her work, analyzing it, criticizing it. No, her art was a private affair between her and her daughter—and maybe Chance. Because Darcy's idea of a portrait for Chance for Christmas wasn't half-bad. With him she felt safe enough to share an important part of herself—her art.

Chapter Nine

❧

"What do you think about putting some more lights up there?" Tanya pointed toward the roof of her house.

Chance stepped back several feet and surveyed it. "You already have twenty-five strands up. Are you trying to outshine the park downtown?"

"I got these lights on sale. I know I probably shouldn't have bought them, but with my new job, I got a raise. I wanted to use a little money to celebrate it. What better way than lots of holidays lights?"

Chance studied Tanya for a moment. Something was wrong. He wasn't sure what, but he felt it in his gut. He took the red string and started for the ladder. "How's the job going?"

"Okay. There's a lot to learn. I'm glad the

seminar is over. Driving back and forth took more time than I thought." While she laid clear lights over the bushes in front, she described her new duties.

Chance half listened to her words. What he really tuned in to was her tone of voice. It sounded as if Tanya had been up for the past several nights and was going through the motions of living on little sleep and a lot of caffeine.

When there was a lull in Tanya's discourse on her new job, he asked, "Is everything okay with Crystal?"

"Sure." Then she launched into an account of her daughter's week at school which Chance already knew from Crystal herself. Tanya described in detail Crystal eating lunch with Grant the day before in the school cafeteria.

He descended the ladder after stringing the lights on the roof then walked to where Tanya continued her task of putting up lights along the porch railing. "Is everything okay with you?"

Her brow crunched into a frown. "Yes, why would you ask? Crystal seems happy. I've got a new job I like."

Kneading the back of his neck, he tried to decide how to put his concerns. "You're acting different. I thought maybe something was wrong." He paused, drew in a deep, fortifying breath and added, "Have you been taking your medication?"

"Why would you ask that?" Anger laced her voice.

He shrugged. It had been over a month since he'd read about manic depression, but Tanya wasn't acting right. He needed to check online, maybe call one of her friends.

He cut the distance between them and brushed his finger under each eye. "Are you sleeping? You've got dark circles under your eyes."

Shrugging away, she moved toward the porch steps. "I just told you that the driving back and forth between Sweetwater and Lexington was more than I anticipated. So naturally I haven't got as much sleep as I usually do." She finished putting up the strand of lights, twisting it around the poles.

Chance watched her hurried movements. He started to say something when she gathered up the few strings left and said, "I think that's all for today. I still have to clean my house." She hoisted the almost-empty box of lights and climbed the stairs to the porch. "Thanks for your help. We'll have to pick Crystal up at the center in two hours."

"Fine. But—"

Tanya opened the front door and disappeared inside. Chance swallowed his words, his mouth hanging open for a few seconds before he quickly closed it.

He strode toward his apartment, removing his cell and punching in Darcy's number.

"Chance, what do you need?"

"I'm worried about Tanya. She's not acting like she usually does. What are some of the signs of manic depression?"

"Not sleeping. Recklessness. Impulsiveness. Too much energy. Talking fast. Poor judgment. Easily distracted. Heightened moods. Irritable and sometimes aggressive. That's some of the symptoms for mania. Do you want them for depression?"

"No. If there's a problem, it's mania. Tanya told me she hasn't been sleeping. The whole morning all she did was talk and talk while she was working. Half the time she would start one string of lights, get distracted and do a new one across the yard. I had to go back and finish up for her. She had so much nervous energy she made me edgy."

"I'll come over. She once told me she wished she could stop taking her medication. She was raised to believe that a pill wasn't the answer to everything."

"Don't, Darcy. Let me take care of it." He hung up before she could protest.

He stood on the small landing into his apartment and stared at the front lawn with every bush, tree and pole covered with lights, not to mention the house. When she switched them on tonight, he'd need a pair of sunglasses. A laugh threatened to erupt until he thought of the seriousness of the situation. He didn't want Crystal to know what was going on and have her worry. He headed back down the stairs to the driveway, then jogged to the back door and pounded on it.

Tanya rushed across the kitchen and flung open the door. "Forget something?" She flashed him a smile and whirled around to hurry to the refrigerator. "Want something to drink? How about some brownies?" She left the refrigerator and rummaged through the pantry.

He took hold of her arms and pulled her away from the cabinet. "What I want is for you to sit and talk with me."

She glanced at her watch then the clock on the wall. "I don't know. Remember we need to get Crystal. I need to make her something to eat before we go to Darcy's farm. Maybe I should make her something to drink, too. She hates apple juice." She checked her watch again.

"There's just not enough time in the day to do everything."

Tugging her away from the pantry, Chance scooted out a chair and sat her in it, then took a seat in front of her so he faced her. He held both of her hands between them and stared at her. She wouldn't meet his gaze.

"I realize you didn't really answer me earlier. Have you been taking your medication lately?"

She averted her head. "Partly."

"What do you mean partly?"

"This week I cut back on my mood stabilizer. With the holidays and my new job, I've had so much to do that I thought if I didn't have to sleep as much I could get—" The color drained from her face. She brought her hand up to her mouth. "What have I done?"

"Nothing that can't be fixed. Why don't you get your medication and take it now? Then call your doctor and check in with him."

She rose and left the kitchen. A moment later she came back in with a bottle in her hand. After speaking with her doctor she took what he prescribed, then eased down onto the chair.

With a shudder, she hugged her arms to her chest. "I wish I didn't have to take the medication."

"I know." He moved his chair closer until their legs pressed together. "You have to think of yourself like a diabetic who can't live without insulin."

"Everything was fine. I thought I could cut back and be fine. I wasn't going to stop taking the medication, just not take as much."

"But you were all over the place. You weren't fine."

Tanya buried her face in her hands. "I'm so ashamed."

The steel case around his emotions cracked open. "Why? You have no reason to be ashamed. You have an illness and you're under a doctor's care. You need medication and counseling to help you live a healthy, happy life. You have done nothing wrong. People deal with all kinds of illnesses every day. Yours happens to be manic depression." He covered her hands and massaged his fingers into her skin, willing his touch to heal her hurt.

She lifted her head, her eyes swimming with tears. "I didn't make a fool of myself out there in the front yard this morning?"

"Nope. But it was obvious to anyone who knows you well that you weren't acting like you usually do."

"My doctor wants to see me on Monday

then have me make an appointment with my counselor."

"Do you want me to go with you?"

She shook her head. "I can do it by myself. As much as I wish things were different, they aren't. I have to accept that. I have no choice because I won't go back to the way I was right after Crystal's accident."

"And if you slip, you've got friends who are here to help."

"Who helps you?"

"I don't—"

She silenced his words with the touch of her fingers against his lips, the warmth of his skin against the tips electrifying. "Everyone needs help from time to time, even you." She pushed the last of her tears back and asked, "If I slip in the future, will you be one of those friends who is here to help me find my way back?"

The question hung in the air between them.

His large hands clasped her smaller ones. "I can't answer that. Probably not. But you have Darcy, Jesse, Beth and Zoey to help you. You have Crystal."

But not you. That hurt worse than the realization she would be on medication for her manic depression for the rest of her life. Her little experiment hadn't worked. She'd known better, but she had wanted so badly to be totally free of her illness.

She pushed a smile through the hurt and said, "Well, at least my yard is decorated for the holidays. Now all we need is the Christmas tree."

"And we're picking that out later this afternoon."

"Yeah, Darcy's latest idea is a good one. I can't wait."

"Good? You aren't the one who will be chopping the tree down."

"True." She squeezed his upper arm. "But you've got the muscles to do the job. I don't." She flexed hers. "Not promising."

"You've got a point there. When do we meet everyone at the farm?"

"In a little over an hour. I volunteered to bring some cookies." She slapped a hand over her mouth. "Oh, no. I forgot. I volunteered to bring some homemade cookies."

"You don't have any?"

"Nope."

Chance rose and held out his hand. "C'mon. We've got an hour until we pick Crystal up at the youth center. I can help you with the cookies. That is, if you have the ingredients."

"You bake?"

He tugged her to her feet. "Nope, but I can follow directions. Lead the way."

The scent of freshly baked chocolate chip cookies saturated the van with its scintillating aroma. After parking in front of the youth center, Tanya hopped down and hurried toward the building with Chance right behind her. The cold, crisp air wrapped its icy fingers around her, prodding her to move even faster. She side-stepped a mound of dirty snow plowed off the sidewalk and mounted the steps.

Inside the warmth of the center chased away the chill gripping her. "Crystal should have finished tutoring Amanda and Brady." Tanya looked up and down the long hall. "I thought she would be out here waiting since we're a little late."

"You called her to let her know we were running behind. Maybe she's in the gym. The Saturday Basketball League is playing a game right now and Grant is one of the players. Maybe she's watching."

"I guess," she murmured, listening to the stomping and shouting coming from the gym. But the hairs on her nape tingled.

For the past month everything had been calm with Crystal as if Holly had decided to stop harassing her daughter. Crystal had even insisted on going to the center without Chance there to watch over her. Now, however, Tanya had second thoughts. She'd asked Crystal to be in the front hall waiting since they were behind schedule.

Chance stared at her for a few seconds. "I'll look in the gym. You take the classrooms on the right. Then I'll check the ones on the left."

Amanda was with her daughter. She would be okay. She was overreacting. She noticed some doors were open, some closed. Those rooms were the ones she would check first.

Tanya opened the door to the nearest room. Empty. She moved to the second one. A group of twelve- and thirteen-year-olds were talking. Her hand shook as she gripped the handle on the third one. For some reason she inched it open quietly. Low voices, furious and sharp, accosted her as she peeked inside.

"We've had enough of you spreading rumors and gossip about Crystal and now Amanda." Eddy stood in a warrior's stance in front of Holly and her friend. On one side of the young man was Jane and on the other Brady. "It's wrong. It's against what Christ taught us is right. Crystal and Amanda have tried to be nice to you this past month and all you've done is make their lives unbearable. Not anymore. We won't let it happen." Eddy gestured toward his friends around him.

Holly pushed against him. "Get out of my way. I'll tell my father."

Eddy crossed his arms over his chest. "Go ahead. And then we'll tell about the graffiti about Crystal and Amanda that you wrote on the girls' bathroom walls here and at school."

"I didn't do it! *She* lies!" Holly pointed toward Crystal sitting in her wheelchair off to the side with Amanda next to her.

"I saw you," Jane said, stepping in front of Eddy. "I expect you to have the walls here at the center cleaned off today and the ones at school on Monday."

"I won't—"

"It isn't negotiable, Holly." Jane held her ground.

"I have friends that—"

"I think you'll discover your 'friends' won't fight this battle with you. You need to take lessons from Crystal on what a good friend is. You aren't one."

Tanya sensed Chance come up behind her. He put his hands on her shoulders and squeezed them. Tears crowded her eyes as she watched the group of teens deal with Crystal's tormentors.

"We will not stand by and watch you hurt our

friend." Eddy walked to Crystal and positioned himself next to her.

When Brady followed, standing beside Amanda, Jane said, "So what's your choice? Leave or take care of your mess."

Holly glared at Crystal, her hands curling and uncurling. A tense silence vibrated the air. Finally Holly huffed and said, "I'll clean it up," then flounced out of the room, throwing a glare at Tanya as she passed her.

Tears ran down Tanya's cheeks, matching the ones that coursed down her daughter's.

The older teens circled Crystal's wheelchair with Eddy saying, "There isn't a place at this center or in this town for a bully. If she bothers you again, Crystal, let me know. There are a group of us dedicated to taking care of people who try to bully. We won't tolerate it."

"But she does have a lot of friends who don't care—"

Eddy knelt in front of Crystal, taking her hand. "No, she doesn't. They just don't know what to do when she bullies someone. Dane is gonna start some classes on bullying and what to do in a situation where you're harassed by a classmate or you witness someone bullying another. If we allow bullying," Eddy pointed to himself, "then it will happen. But if we don't, we can stop it."

Jane grinned. "Hey, kid, I haven't been watching you grow up for nothing. I'm your friend. Come to me if there's a problem. What are friends for but to help?"

Tanya turned away from the scene, a lump lodged in her throat. She knew Crystal had seen her, but she wanted to give her daughter some privacy with her friends. Besides, she needed time to gather her own composure after what she had witnessed. Friends coming to the aid of a friend in trouble. Crystal would be all right as long as she had good friends around her. And so would she as Chance had pointed out earlier that day. Even if he left—and she knew he would—she would be all right. Her heart would break, but she would make it because she had the support she needed in place with her friends and the love of the Lord.

Tanya waited by the front door with Chance. She saw Holly and her friend go into the girls' bathroom with some cleaning supplies. The anger in the teen's expression saddened her.

Chance stared at the restroom door through which the two girls had disappeared. "Bullies aren't born. Holly was made. Remember when I witnessed her dad yelling at her and telling her how stupid she was? They are not the perfect family everyone's been led to believe. As I told you after the Holiday Light Ceremony, I have a feeling Holly learned the tactics of a bully from her father."

"That doesn't surprise me after what he's tried to do with you."

"But the tactics aren't working with me. I don't care what he thinks, and I have friends to help me. Jim and Wilbur are nothing compare to the predators in prison."

"Most people in Sweetwater are seeing what you're doing. Some of their children are getting the help they need in math because of you."

"It's not just me tutoring." He straightened as he saw Crystal driving her wheelchair toward them. "Your daughter has a natural talent for teaching."

"I'm discovering my daughter has a lot of talents. She may not be able to walk, but God has gifted her with so much." Tanya pushed open the front door. "You all ready? The best trees are probably gone by now."

Crystal with a huge grin on her face headed out into the cold. "Nah. I bet Darcy is waiting for us to arrive before they start."

When everyone was settled in the van and the heater blasted warm air, Tanya backed out of her parking space and drove toward Darcy's family farm. Anticipation of the fun to come hummed through her veins. For the first time in months she experienced hope that her daughter would be all right. Crystal might have to deal with being in a wheelchair the rest of her life, but then people often had something they had to deal with their whole life—like her manic depression.

Fifteen minutes later Tanya parked next to a horse barn, noticing that they were the last to arrive at Darcy's. Several other vehicles were already there, which meant everyone was inside the brown structure, waiting for them just as Crystal had said. In the barn some of the horses were saddled while others were being readied to ride.

Tanya noticed that everyone had horses. "I don't know why I agreed to this. I don't ride."

Darcy lumbered over to them. "I've been having some contractions so I'm giving you the sled. Dad and Sean are gonna get our tree while Joshua and I stay back, just in case."

Tanya pointed at her friend's large round stomach. "Just in case you have the baby today? You should have called and canceled this outing."

"No way. We need a tree and we have a whole forest of Christmas trees waiting for everyone to choose one for their living rooms." Darcy smiled at Crystal. "Sorry, but you have to ride with your mom and Chance. Though it's probably a good thing. You can keep those two in line."

Tanya sidled next to Chance and whispered, "Okay, do I look as red as Crystal's scarf?"

He studied her—a mistake to ask him, Tanya decided because the heat intensified on her face.

His dimpled grin appeared. "Your friends have a refreshing candor."

"I wasn't gonna call their meddling refreshing."

"Let's go, Mom, Chance. Everyone's ready to go. The sled's out back."

Sean wheeled Crystal toward the back doors. A blast of cold swept into the barn when he opened them. Samuel mounted after Craig got on his horse and Allie rode behind him. Beth stayed behind because of her pregnancy. Jane climbed into her saddle, her animal tied next to Jesse and Nick's. Nate and Cindy were already on two small mares which their parents were going to lead. Darcy's dad was at the front of the group with Sean next to him. Zoey and Dane were the last to get on their geldings. Joshua handed up Mandy to Zoey and Dane took Tara. Blake hopped onto his own horse.

"When you get the perfect tree and cut it

down, head back here. There will be hot chocolate and sweets waiting," Darcy announced to the group while Tanya ascended the sled.

Chance lifted Crystal out of her wheelchair and placed her next to Tanya. Then he climbed up onto the sled and took the reins. "Ready? Joshua told me a great place to look for the perfect tree."

All the horses and riders headed out into the snow-covered pasture near the barn. Chance directed the two horses pulling the sled along the road that led to the back part of the farm. Tanya wrapped the wool blanket around their legs, then snuggled down into the warmth created by being sandwiched between her daughter and Chance.

The tinkles of bells, hanging off the sled, echoed through the cold air as they glided farther away from the barn. Gray clouds roiled across the sky, churning and eating up the blue. The wind, scented with the hint of snow, picked up.

Away from people and animals the cover of snow was unbroken, a white carpet lying over the ground with trees and bushes poking up out of it. In the distance she saw the pines that Chance was heading toward. Some shot up toward the sky, tall, majestic. No way one of them would get inside her house. Maybe a seven-foot tree, she thought, excited at the prospects of sharing the holidays with Chance.

He pulled back on the reins and stopped the horses at the edge of a copse that fed into a larger forest bordering the lake. "Anything call to you?"

Crystal giggled. "Nothing's calling 'cut me,' but I like that one."

Tanya looked toward the four-foot tree that stood slightly apart from the others as if it had been shunned because its scraggy branches would hold only a third, possibly a half, of her ornaments. "Don't you want something bigger? Our living room could take a tree up to maybe seven feet tall."

Her daughter cocked her head to the side and studied the scrawny pine. "Nope. It needs us. No one else would pick it." She turned toward Tanya, excitement gleaming in her eyes. "It's small enough that we could dig it up instead of cutting it down and maybe after Christmas plant it in our yard. Do you think we could?" Her hopeful gaze traveled from Tanya to Chance.

He peered at Crystal for a few seconds, then slid his regard back toward the pine, its limbs gently waving in the light breeze. "I'll have to come back. All I have is an ax."

"Will you, Chance? Please?"

Her daughter's enthusiasm infused each of her words, making Tanya excited, too. "I can help. We can come back tomorrow after church."

"I can try, but it might not make it. I might not be able to get all of its root system."

"Maybe Joshua knows what to do. He loves to work in his yard." Tanya surveyed the under-sized Christmas tree and warmed to the idea of loading its branches down with the ornaments that meant the most to her and Crystal.

Chance prodded the horses forward and swung the sled in a wide circle. "I'll ask him when we get to the barn. We can all come back tomorrow afternoon if Darcy will loan us the sled again. I don't think this snow will melt anytime soon."

"It's supposed to snow tonight. What if we can't come back?" Crystal threw a glance over her shoulder at her tree.

"The van has snow tires. If we can't come tomorrow, we will as soon as possible since Christmas is only two weeks away." Tanya scanned the darkening clouds, a few flakes falling. She held out a gloved hand and caught a flake which melted immediately.

Tanya tugged the blanket up and made sure that Crystal was completely covered. She snuggled closer to Chance, placed her arm around her daughter's shoulder and pulled her against her side to warm her as much as she could. The temperature in the past hour they had been out had dropped at least five degrees. The wind gusted.

"That hot chocolate sounds so good right now," Crystal said, shivering.

"It's only a few more minutes." Chance directed the horses onto the road that led to the barn. "I wonder what the others got."

Five minutes later Chance brought the horses to a halt right outside the barn's back doors. He hopped down and went inside to retrieve Crystal's wheelchair.

Dane helped him get Crystal out of the sled. "Darcy and Joshua were gone when we got back a little while ago. She went to the hospital. Lizzie and Beth were waiting for us and insisted we have the hot chocolate and sweets. Darcy doesn't want us all to go to the hospital. She wants us to wait until she calls. It could be a false alarm."

"This could be it. She's only a couple of weeks early. If she has the baby now, she won't spend Christmas in the hospital. She told me once she was afraid she would have her baby on Christmas Day and miss the celebration." Tanya climbed down from the sled and followed Crystal, Dane and Chance into the barn.

Inside everyone was back except Nick and Jesse's family. Beth helped Lizzie, Darcy's stepmother, pour three mugs of hot chocolate, then carried them over to Tanya, Chance and Crystal.

After tying his pine to the roof of his car, Samuel and his son came in from the front. "Where's your tree?" the reverend asked Chance, taking his own mug from his wife's hand.

"Still in the ground. I'm coming back to dig it up."

"That's ambitious. The ground may be too frozen to do it."

"I've got to try. Crystal fell in love with this one and wants to plant it in the yard after Christmas. It hasn't been that cold until lately."

"And winter has now hit with a vengeance." Tanya joined Chance and Samuel, cradling the heated mug between her hands. She relished the warm steam, laced with the scent of chocolate, wafting to her face.

Shamus Flanaghan's cell phone rang. After he answered it, he said to the group, "It's official. She's gonna have the baby tonight, God willing."

"Let's say a prayer for Darcy and Joshua."

Samuel moved into the middle of the circle and bowed his head.

Tanya clasped Crystal's and Chance's hands, remembering back to when her daughter was born.

"Lord, You are about to give a loving couple another child. Please protect them and be with Darcy and the new baby through her birth and the days to follow. Also, help Joshua to give Darcy the support and encouragement she will need tonight. We will be here to teach their new daughter Your importance and the love You and Your son, Jesus, have for us."

Amid the others' *amens*, Tanya heard Chance's clear strong voice utter the word. Her heart swelled with the sound. He had attended church with her and Crystal the past two weeks. His presence added a joy and hope that she hadn't felt until he had started going to church. Maybe he was ready to forgive and put his trust in God again.

Jesse and her family came into the barn. "Darcy's in labor?" she asked, looking around at the smiles on everyone's faces.

"Yes, they just wheeled her into delivery." Shamus hugged his grandson to his side.

"Well, what are we standing around here for? Let's get to the hospital." Jesse nudged her husband who dragged the tree they selected behind him.

"The staff isn't gonna know what hit them when we come," Tanya said with a laugh.

"Nah. Remember the last time? Granted, we have added a few more people, but I think they expect us to all turn out." Beth looped her arm through Samuel's.

"We've practically doubled in size." Jesse held up her hand, counting off the people as she named them. "There's Samuel, his children, Chance, Dane."

"Just wait until you have yours." Tanya started for the front doors. "Less than six months to go."

Jesse moaned. "Don't remind me. Six months of gaining weight and looking like a beached whale."

Chance opened the massive double doors. "You can drop me by the apartment on the way to the hospital."

Tanya halted halfway to the van. "You don't want to come and celebrate the birth of Darcy and Joshua's daughter?"

"I don't belong. It's a family—well, not a family affair but...you know what I mean?"

She placed her hand on her waist, aware that it was beginning to snow a little harder. A couple of flakes caught on her eyelashes and she blinked. "No, I don't understand. You're a part of this group. Darcy would be disappointed if you weren't there."

"I don't—"

"Going by the house is out of my way. I want to get to the hospital before it really starts snowing." Tanya walked to the back to operate the lift for Crystal.

When she secured her daughter in the van, she moved around to the driver's side and slipped in. "Besides, you are at my mercy. You go where I go."

Chance opened his mouth to say something, but no words came out. He pressed it closed and stared straight ahead.

Chapter Ten

At the end of the church pew Chance sat between Tanya and Crystal in her wheelchair. He stifled a yawn as Samuel rose to give his sermon. Being up half the night took its toll on him, especially when he didn't sleep the other half because of the woman sitting next to him and her insistence that he accompany her and Crystal to the hospital. To be a part of Darcy and Joshua's celebration of their new daughter. To be a part of the close friendship the five families had for each other. No matter how much Tanya wanted it, he was still an outsider. He would always be the outsider.

But for a few minutes last night, it had been nice to wonder what it would feel like being a part of this close-knit group of friends.

As Samuel began to talk about hope, using

the illustration of the birth of Joshua and Darcy's daughter, Tanya slipped her hand over his, sending him a smile. Deep in her eyes he saw a connection forged between them with the shared experiences of the past few months. A strong urge to tug his hand away deluged him with panic.

Then Samuel's words came to Chance, calming him. "Jesus died for us. God gave us hope with His Son's resurrection. Peter best said it, 'Blessed be the God and Father of our Lord Jesus Christ, which according to His abundant mercy hath begotten us again unto a lively hope by the resurrection of Jesus Christ from the dead.' Remember those words when you think there is no hope in your life. Remember what Christ went through for us in the end, all because He loved us. Believe in Him and you will always have that hope."

Was it that simple? Chance wanted it to be. Mentally recapping his life, he needed to do something. He needed a purpose. Soon his job would be done here. Then what?

As everyone around him rose for the final song, Chance stood and joined in with Crystal and Tanya. The calm that had started with Samuel's sermon spread outward to encompass his whole body. By the time Chance left the pew and followed Crystal and Tanya toward the exit where Samuel greeted his congregation, Chance latched onto the feelings developing inside him. He liked those feelings—the peace. He hadn't had that in a long time.

"Nice service, Samuel," Chance said and shook his friend's hand.

"After being up most of the night, I wasn't sure I would be able to string more than a few sentences together."

"Well, you managed just fine."

Samuel studied him. "Did they give you something to think on?"

He nodded.

"Then this has been a good day." Samuel turned to Tanya and Crystal. "Are you all staying for refreshments?"

"For a few minutes. We still have to go get our Christmas tree this afternoon." Although Tanya answered Samuel's question, her gaze never left Chance's face.

The second they were out in the church foyer, she stopped him while Crystal continued toward the rec hall. Off from the others milling about, Tanya leaned close and whispered, "You felt God's presence, didn't you?"

"Yes."

She beamed. "He hasn't abandoned you.

Let's go get something to drink and eat. We've got hard physical work ahead of us this afternoon. I want the Christmas tree up and decorated this evening. Think that's possible?"

He chuckled. "Yeah. I definitely think it is."

Later that evening, a fire burned in the fireplace. The scent of wood permeated Tanya's living room. Cozy. Romantic. With only the lights from the Christmas tree and the blaze, for a while, the rest of the world didn't exist. There were only the three of them—Crystal, Chance and her. Charlie slept in front of the fire, oblivious to what was going on around him.

Tanya stood back and surveyed the small pine with so many ornaments on its limbs that they drooped, the bottom ones almost to the carpet. "I won't be surprised if one morning we wake up and find all the balls have slid off the tree." Her head tilted to the side, she tapped her finger against her chin.

"We can always remove some." Crystal positioned her wheelchair next to the pine and reached for a cardboard circle colored with red and green markers and a silver glittered glob in the middle.

"No! Not that one. Remember you made that for me in first grade."

Crystal went for another homemade one, and Tanya shook her head. After going through several more, her daughter blew out a breath, her bangs lifting.

"Mom, half of these are ugly."

"Not to me. They're precious. There's a story behind every ornament on that tree."

Chance moved forward, his arm brushing against Tanya's. "We had ornaments like that."

The roughened edge to his voice riveted Tanya's attention to his face. Pain etched his features. "Where are they? Maybe we can get another small tree and you can have one in your apartment."

"No!" he said as forcefully as Tanya a moment ago.

"You need something." She itched to smooth away the creases in his expression.

"Why? I'm perfectly content to come look at yours when I need a Christmas fix. Besides, I don't want anyone to go to any trouble. I don't spend enough time there."

Crystal yawned loudly. "I'm tired. We did a lot today. Since I have some homework I need to finish, I'd better do it before I fall asleep. Good night, Chance, Mom."

"Night, Crystal." Chance's gaze drilled into Tanya's.

"If you need some help, let me know, honey."
Tanya refused to look away from him.

When the sound of the wheelchair faded
down the hall, Tanya asked, "What happened
to your Christmas decorations?" He would
never get on with his life if he didn't deal with
his loss, every aspect of it. She knew; she'd
been there with Tom.

Pain still reflected in his expression, Chance
pivoted away and walked to the fireplace,
staring down at the flames as they licked the
huge logs in the grate. He stuffed his hands
into the front pockets of his black jeans.
Focusing on the plaid pattern of his flannel shirt
for a moment, Tanya gave him some time to
bring his emotions under control.

As his rigid stance dissolved into a relaxed
one, Tanya strode to him and laid her hand on
his arm. "What happened?"

After taking in a calming breath, he visibly
swallowed and said, "Ruth's parents took them,
along with most of her and my daughter's things."

"Why haven't you gotten them back?"

"I don't want them. The picture I have in my
apartment is all I need. I can't bring either one
back. They are in my past and as much as I wish
they hadn't been murdered, I can't change what
happened." His gaze sought hers. "Today, for

the first time in a long while, I felt hope when I listened to Samuel's sermon. I don't want to let that feeling go."

"Then don't. I have fond and loving memories of Tom, but I have had to learn to move on with my life. I can't afford for Crystal's sake to live in the past."

His smile deepened the dimples in his cheeks and the pain disappeared completely from his gaze. "I'm working on it. I enjoyed decorating your—" he looked at the small pine "—uh, tree this evening."

She basked in the teasing that shone in his eyes. "It's not too bad. I'm beginning to think like Crystal. That tree was calling out for someone to take it, and after Christmas, we can plant it in our backyard so we can remember this holiday for years to come." *I know I will.* Chance's presence made the first Christmas since Tom's death bearable to her and Crystal. "I've got some more hot chocolate. Want a refill?"

"Sure. But you sit and I'll go get it. I know my way around your kitchen."

Tanya settled on the couch before the fireplace with the tree off to the side, listening to Chance rummaging around in her kitchen. When he reappeared with the two mugs, steam floating upward, her stomach flip-flopped with his look that said he only had eyes for her. She wanted to savor this moment so she could revisit it in the future when Chance left Sweetwater. If only he would stay, then— She shook that wish from her mind. She had to be practical for once and steel her heart as much as possible against the hurt that would follow his departure.

Pausing in front of her, Chance held her mug out. She slipped her fingers around the warm ceramic, brushing against his. He eased down next to her, close but not touching. All Tanya wanted to do was feather her lips across his, be surrounded by his embrace. But she stayed where she was and concentrated on taking one sip, then another of her hot chocolate.

"I love chocolate, and this is great on a cold night," she said to break the silence after a few minutes.

He placed his mug on the coffee table, half his drink gone. "You get no complaints from me."

Tired from a long, productive day, she set her mug next to his, relaxed back against the cushion and watched the flames dancing in the fireplace, the red-orange blaze mesmerizing. Her eyelids slid closed. From afar she heard the crackling of the fire, felt the warmth it generated....

"Tanya, we'd better call it a night."

Chance's voice penetrated the fog that shrouded her mind. Tanya blinked her eyes open and found herself pressed against his side on the couch, his arm along the back of the cushion, her head resting on his shoulder. What a great way to spend an evening. Content, she didn't move for a good minute. Then slowly she straightened.

"Yes, you're right. Six o'clock tomorrow morning will come soon enough." Tanya glanced at her watch and realized she must have dozed about fifteen minutes, cuddled in his arms. That thought sent her heart beating a shade faster.

Chance unfolded his long length and rose, then tugged her up. He wound his arms around her waist and brought her near. "As much as I'm enjoying myself, I agree. Tomorrow starts a long work week."

He bent his head a few inches closer, and Tanya could smell the chocolate on his breath. "Thank you for digging up the tree for us. It really is a nice one. Just don't tell Crystal I said so. I love how protective she is over it."

"My lips are sealed."

Her gaze fixed upon those lips, and she couldn't take her eyes off them. She wanted him to kiss her. Every part of her screamed for it.

Slowly his mouth settled over hers, ending her frustration. His kiss stamped her his, even if he would never know how much she really cared about him. She would never forget this time with him.

As he deepened the kiss, she melted against him, clinging to him. With each second that passed, she became more and more connected to him on a level that left her shaken. He was a man who had suffered greatly and was trying to put his life back together. And today he had taken the first step in his journey back to the Lord.

Chance pulled away and firmly put some space between them. His breathing was short and raspy. His look nearly undid her all over again. It proclaimed the connection in his glittering blue depths. Her mind wiped blank, she stared at him as he collected himself, the rapid rise and fall of his chest slowing.

"I need to leave. See you tomorrow," he finally said in a voice rough, intense with emotion.

She didn't follow him to the door but just watched him stalk toward the front hallway. A few seconds later she heard the door shut. She pressed her hands to her cheeks. The warmth beneath her palms seared the past few minutes into her mind.

Their relationship had moved to another level tonight. She could no longer kid herself that she and Chance were just good friends. The kiss they had shared made a mockery of that. She had wanted more, and in his expression she'd seen he had, too.

Chance stormed into his apartment and headed for the closet. He dragged out his duffel bag, emptied the top drawer of the chest and stuffed his T-shirts, jeans and socks into his only piece of luggage. Halfway back to the closet to get his pants and shirts, he halted.

Staring at the overflowing duffel bag, he realized how many material items he had acquired in the past three months. But most of all, he realized he couldn't run away. He wasn't a man who went back on a promise, even though he had made it to himself. He would stay through the holidays and make sure that Tanya and Crystal were cared for.

He just couldn't kiss her again.

Too dangerous.

Chance shoved the bag over and sank down onto the couch that converted into a bed. Why had he ruined a wonderful day by kissing her like that? Why had he poured his heart into it?

I find a few moments of peace earlier in

church, and all of a sudden I'm wanting to build a life with Tanya and Crystal. Leaning forward, he buried his hands in his hair and stared at the floor. He hadn't come to Sweetwater to get involved romantically with anyone, especially Tom's wife.

He'd had a family once. He couldn't go through losing another. *Lord, I'm asking for Your help. Stop these feelings for Tanya from growing. I don't want to care about her like that. I want to help her, then I want to leave. Please, God that is the only way.*

After finishing the last sip of coffee, Tanya cupped her chin in her hand and rested her elbow on her kitchen table. "Jesse, Christmas is ten days away and I can't think of a thing to get Chance. He's gonna have dinner with Crystal and me on Christmas Day. He's gotta have something under the tree. Buying him something like clothes doesn't convey what I want to convey."

Jesse relaxed back in the chair opposite her. "And what *do* you want to convey?"

"I…" Tanya toyed with the rim of her mug, running her finger around and around it. What did she want to convey? Everything she had looked at in the store hadn't seemed right. She didn't know why but each time she had gone shopping she had come away empty-handed. "I'm not sure. I guess I want to thank him for helping out with Crystal."

Jesse quirked a brow. "Is that all?"

She sat up straight. "What's that supposed to mean?"

"You're only thinking of Crystal?"

"Okay, I want to thank him for being my friend, too."

"Just a friend?"

Tanya huffed. "Don't you start matchmaking, Jesse Blackburn. We are friends. Nothing more." She had to keep reminding herself of that in spite of the kiss they had shared recently, or when he left, she would fall apart. She'd done enough of that in the past four years to last a lifetime.

"For being just friends, you two have been spending a lot of time together lately."

"Look, we haven't even seen each other since last Sunday when we decorated the tree. He's been busy. I've been busy. We haven't had a chance even to jog because of the weather."

"That's only five days."

"Six. Today's Saturday." Tanya stood and took her mug over to the sink, needing to move, to do something to keep herself from dwelling on the six *long* days she hadn't seen Chance except in passing. Crystal had seen him at the center a lot more than she had.

"Today isn't over yet." Jesse brought her mug to the counter and lounged back against it.

"Where did he and Nick go?"

"Can't say."

Tanya spun around and faced her with a hand plunked on her waist. "Jesse, you can't keep a secret from me."

"Sorry. He needed Nick's SUV. That's all I know. They wouldn't even tell me."

"He could have borrowed my van."

"He thought you might need it." Her friend crossed her arms and tilted her head to the side. "Now, back to your problem. What to get Chance for Christmas. Does he have any hobbies?"

"Besides jogging, which I don't consider a hobby, I can't think of anything. He's either working or helping out at the center or—" Tanya glanced out the window over the sink "—helping Crystal and me."

"Well, I guess you two are his hobby." Jesse laughed.

"You aren't helping."

"Sorry. Back to your dilemma. Why not do something for him?"

"What? His apartment is sparse and always

clean. He—" Two ideas began to form in her mind. Tanya turned away, taking Jesse's mug and rinsing it out before putting both of them in the dishwasher. "Come to think of it, there is something I could do."

"What?"

"He needs his own tree. His apartment might as well be a motel room. I have a key and both him and Nick are gonna be gone all afternoon. Want to help me get a small tree and decorate it? I have leftover ornaments that I didn't have room for on mine."

Jesse pushed away from the counter. "Sure. I'm game. Do you think he'll be okay with you using your key?"

"He knows I have it and doesn't mind. Personally I don't even think he sees that apartment as his place. I just want to spread a little joy. He's made the past few months so much easier for Crystal and me." Although he'd declared last Sunday he didn't spend much time in his apartment, she wanted him to enjoy the holidays even when he was there.

"Well, then we've got some work to do."

Later that afternoon, Tanya paced her kitchen, glancing at the clock every few minutes. Restless energy surged through her. She couldn't sit. She couldn't do anything until she knew what Chance thought of his Christmas tree.

Reflecting back over the day, she recalled the letter she had seen lying on his kitchen table from the district attorney in Louisville about the trial of the man who had killed his wife and daughter. While setting the box of ornaments down, she had glimpsed the date of the trial before she realized what she was looking at. She'd quickly averted her gaze, but guilt had taken hold of her. Although she had known about the impending trial, seeing the date written in black and white made it very real and looming.

At first she had wanted to leave and hoped that Chance didn't figure out that she'd been in his apartment. But the damage had been done. She'd seen the letter and couldn't ignore what Chance would be going through in less than a month. All the old hurts would be exposed again. The least she could do was give him something festive to look at when he awakened each morning—and her apology for intruding.

Nick's SUV pulled into the driveway as it started to get dark. In the headlights Tanya saw snowflakes falling. The roads had been finally cleared stoday, and now it looked as if it would start all over again. She wasn't distressed one bit. She loved the cold, the snow. Its soft white blanket made everything quiet and pristine as though God had laid a cover of pureness upon the earth.

She closed the blinds, turned away from the window and stared at her kitchen. She chewed her thumbnail. *Should I go see him now? Or wait to see if he comes over here?*

She didn't know what to do. Fifteen minutes later when Chance hadn't come to see her, she knew she had to go to him. Throwing on a sweater, she hurried across the yard and quickly climbed the stairs. Snow coated her hair and clothes as it began to fall harder. In another half an hour she would have to go pick up Crystal at the youth center. But for the time being, she needed to see Chance.

The door stood ajar a few inches. She knocked on it, causing it to swing inward a couple of more inches. Although Chance hadn't responded to her knock, she glimpsed him sitting on the couch, staring at the tree as though in a trance, an expression of disbelief on his face.

"Chance?"

He blinked but didn't glance toward her.

"I'm sorry. I shouldn't have done this. I

shouldn't have come here without you knowing. I know what you said last time—"

He finally twisted completely toward her, a sheen in his eyes. His look, full of awe and something she couldn't quite identify, snatched her words and breath.

She stepped into his apartment and closed the cold and snow out. "I wanted to surprise you."

One corner of his mouth tilted upward. "That you did," he murmured, his voice thick.

"Then you aren't upset?"

He started to say something but had to clear his throat before he proceeded. "Upset? Until I came to Sweetwater, I hadn't had many nice things done for me in a long time. That all changed the minute I stepped off that bus. You and your friends have welcomed me as though I was one of you." He rose and waved his hand toward the lit tree. "And now this."

"Then you like it?" She took another step farther into the room.

"Like it? I love the gesture, Tanya. If you had asked me, I would have told you no. In fact, I did. I didn't think I needed anything for the holidays. But when I walked in here and saw the tree, I realized I was wrong." Swallowing visibly, he made his way to her but stopped short of touching her.

She yearned for his arms to be around her, but he had kept his distance the past six days because of the kiss they had shared Sunday night. He didn't have to come right out and tell her but she knew. He didn't want to take their relationship beyond friendship, and she had to respect his wishes. She was determined to enjoy what he could offer her and mourn his loss when he left—not one minute before.

She smiled. "Good. It was a spur-of-the-moment plan. Jesse was over here, and I decided that you needed your very own tree after helping Crystal and me with ours. So Jesse helped me with it."

"A few of those ornaments look familiar."

"They should. They're the ones I couldn't use. I hope you don't mind my castoffs."

He peered at the three-foot pine sitting in the middle of his kitchen table with small twinkling lights and a few homemade balls interspersed among gold and red glittery ones hanging from the tree's small branches. "Not at all."

"I did buy that star at the top when I got the tree. I knew it would look perfect where it's sitting."

The gold sequined star blinked on and off, its soft light sending out a radiance that shone down on the whole small pine. Chance walked the few feet to the table and fingered the star.

"My own Star of Bethlehem, right here in my apartment."

"It can be left on separately from the strand of lights."

"Do you think it will help me find my way home?" Chance's gaze fell to the letter not far from the tree. "Did you see they set the date for the trial?"

Suddenly, all emotion fled his voice, and Tanya shivered. "Yes," she whispered as she realized she could say nothing else but the truth.

"I knew it would be soon after the first of the year. But until you see it on paper, it's still an abstract event that will happen sometime in the future."

The heaviness in her heart threatened to cut off her next breath. She'd thought the same thing. She drew in deeply and said, "Chance, I'll help you any way I can. That's the least I can do for all you've done for me and Crystal."

He flinched as though she had hit him. Averting his face, he folded the letter, strode to a drawer and laid it inside.

Something coiled in her stomach. The tightness in her chest expanded. "Don't shut me out. Please." She remembered the times Tom had and what it had led to: her husband turning his anger outward and burning down horse barns.

If only she could have reached Tom in time, maybe then things would have been different.

Chance pivoted. "What do you want me to say? The trial has been set. I knew it was coming. It really was no big surprise." Scanning the apartment as though searching for a way to escape, he said, "Where's Crystal?"

He was so good at letting her see small glimpses inside him, then slamming the door. Tanya wanted to demand he let her help him. But then that never worked. If he wasn't ready, nothing she did would make a difference. "She's at the center. I've got to pick her up—" she checked her watch "—now. I tolsd Dane I would help with cleanup after the holiday party. It should be over soon."

"I'll ride with you."

She walked toward his door. "You don't have to."

He leaned around her and turned the knob. "In case you didn't notice when you came up here, it's snowing. I would feel better if you would humor me and let me tag along."

She shrugged and said, "Sure," then darted out into the gently falling snow. "I just need to get my heavy coat."

Fifteen minutes later, Tanya pulled into the handicapped parking space right in front of the youth center. She and Chance hurried up the steps and into the warm building. A few teens and their parents headed out of the gym, bundled up against the cold. Wilbur Thompson, with his grandson next to him, nodded at Tanya while he glared at Chance.

In spite of the icy greeting, Chance said, "Good evening, Wilbur, Tyler."

Wilbur snorted. "There's nothing good about it. It's snowing *again*. This has got to set some kind of record for us."

As the older man passed them in the foyer, Chance asked, "Do you need any help?"

For a step, Wilbur looked surprised by the offer, then he covered it by wrapping his scarf around his neck and murmuring, "No, Tyler can help me."

"Just let me know if you do." Chance started forward, nearing the large double doors.

"You may win Wilbur over before long," Tanya whispered as she heard the Christmas music coming from the gym.

"I don't know if that's possible, but it won't be because I didn't try. There are still a few holdouts, but thanks to you and your friends, most people have accepted my presence here at the center."

"I'm glad it doesn't bother you working around teens."

He paused, his hand on the swinging door. "Because of Haley? I can't go through life avoiding kids who are the same age as she. If my daughter were alive, she would have loved a place like this." He pushed the door open and moved into the gym.

Tanya followed him. Three months ago she wasn't so sure Chance had felt that way. He'd been a little leery of Crystal at the beginning. Now she realized why. Crystal and Haley, if she had lived, were only a year apart in age.

Tanya searched the crowd of teens still at the holiday party and found her daughter with Amanda, Jane and Grant at one of the tables. The sound of Crystal's laughter sweetened the air as Tanya walked toward her. Chance went in the other direction to see Dane.

"Mom, you're early."

"No, I'm a little late."

Crystal looked down at her watch. "I guess you are. I didn't realize it was so late."

"Hello, Mrs. Bolton. We were talking about the presents Crystal gave us." Grant held up a caricature of himself, showing him playing basketball with his head twice its normal size and his jersey number huge on the front. "Isn't it neat?"

"Yes." Tanya looked at her daughter. So that

was what she had been working so hard on for the past few weeks.

"And here's mine." Jane showed her picture, which showcased Samuel's daughter's talent as an artist. "I'm gonna have to do this."

Tanya saw others as some teenagers came over to thank Crystal. In each caricature her daughter had taken one of the teens' talents and played it up. Sean's was working with computers. Nate's and Craig's were their band. Amanda's was talking on the phone.

"I need to check about cleaning up. I just wanted to let you know I was here," Tanya said.

"We'll be right here." Jane took a sip of her hot chocolate. "Dad and Beth are in the kitchen, cleaning up."

Tanya made her way to the kitchen where Samuel, Beth and Zoey were working. "Need any help in here?"

All three glanced at her and shook their heads while Zoey said, "Got everything under control. You might check with Dane."

Back in the gym Tanya saw Dane and Chance directing some of the youths in cleaning up the trash left on the tables. More of the teenagers were leaving. Relieved they would be home before the snow caused too much trouble on the roads, Tanya walked toward Chance. She peered at Crystal and Amanda, who had begun to pick up the discarded paper cups, and glimpsed Holly stop by her daughter. Tanya tensed and made a detour toward Crystal. She wouldn't allow that teen to ruin her daughter's mood and this successful holiday party.

As Tanya neared Holly from behind, she heard the teenager say, "You're really good at drawing. Thanks for the picture."

Before Tanya could reach Crystal, Holly left, the caricature in the girl's hand. All Tanya could make out of Holly's picture was that the teen was portrayed in her cheerleading outfit with pompoms.

What her daughter had done touched Tanya. Her throat tightened. "You drew a caricature for everyone, even Holly?"

"Well, the ones who come regularly, and those I knew would be here tonight at the party," Crystal said, peering after Holly as she slipped out of the gym. "She thanked me."

"I heard."

"For the past few weeks Holly has avoided me. I almost didn't draw her, but that's not what Jesus taught us. If I believe in Him then I can't ignore His Word." Her daughter's mouth lifted in a sassy grin. "Even though I was sorely tempted. After I finished last night, I knew it was the right thing to do. Now I'm glad I did it."

"Is everything okay here?" Chance asked, approaching them. "I saw Holly talking to you."

Throwing a glance over her shoulder toward Grant helping Eddy clean up, Crystal smiled. "Yeah, everything is great!" Then she drove toward the large trash can to deposit the paper goods she had collected.

Obviously Grant Foster wasn't unaware of her daughter any longer. More and more when she came to pick Crystal up at the youth center, she would find her talking with Grant. Perhaps he was discovering Crystal's inner beauty as others were. "She continues to amaze me. My daughter gave Holly a gift."

"And how did Holly feel about it?" Chance moved to the nearest table and held the plastic bag open while Tanya dumped the remains of the party into it.

"She was okay about it."

"I guess Eddy and Jane's intervention helped. If more people would stand up and say no to someone bullying another, then we wouldn't have as much of a problem as we do."

Tanya walked to the next table and began

cleaning up. "You were right. Bullies aren't born, they are made."

"And after what I saw between Holly and her father, I can imagine where the girl learned her ways."

"Jim Proctor has always thrown his weight around, steamrolling over others." She dropped some more trash into the plastic bag.

"Maybe it isn't too late to teach his daughter there are better ways to interact with peers than to harass them and make fun of them."

"When's Dane starting the antibullying classes?"

"After the new year."

"Do you think anyone will come?"

Chance shrugged. "We have to start somewhere. Even if it means there are only a handful who take the class, it's a beginning."

"We?" Tanya completed removing the used paper goods from the last table. "You sound pretty vested in this."

"I did some research and found the program Dane's going to use. That's all of my participation."

"Because you won't be here?" Tanya held her breath waiting for the reply she knew was going to come.

"Yes."

Chapter Eleven

From across Jesse's large living room Christmas Eve, Tanya watched Chance interact with Dane, Nick and Samuel. The ease with which he fit in with the other men didn't surprise her. He was the same kind of man as her friends' husbands—caring, loving and ethical. Her friends were blessed to have found such men. She didn't envy them their happy marriage; she just wished she was as blessed.

Ever since she and Chance had cleaned up at the youth center after the party, she couldn't get out of her mind that he had told her yet again he was leaving soon. The very thought brought such intense, sad emotions to the foreground. Chance deserved some happiness; she deserved some. Why couldn't he see she would be good for him?

"You're drooling," Jesse whispered close to her ear.

"Am I that transparent?" Tanya turned her attention to her friends standing near her.

"Written all over your face, so if you don't want him to know you need to get better at hiding your feelings." Zoey took a bite of a small sandwich square with cream cheese and cucumber. "This is good, Jesse."

That's it! If she didn't risk her heart and tell him how she felt, how was she ever going to know if she and Chance might work out? She needed to find a time soon to let him know she loved him. There, she'd admitted it. *I love Chance! I want to make a life with him.*

Now to convince him she was the right woman for him. Even if he needed more time to heal, she understood that and would give it to him. She just didn't want him to move away. Her gaze drifted back to Chance, his face lit with laughter, the hard lines of life almost gone.

He may not know it yet, but this is his home now. Every time she looked at him, she saw it in his relaxed stance, the humor in his eyes, the peace that he conveyed.

"I'm thinking if we want Tanya to participate in our conversation, we need to drag Chance over here to join us," Beth said.

Tanya exaggerated a pout and faced her friends. "I had to suffer through you all going all dreamy eyed over your husbands so you will just have to put up with me doing it."

"Ah, there, she has admitted it finally. Congratulations." Jesse patted her on the back.

As Beth and Zoey offered their congratulations, Tanya said, "Shh. You'll have everyone in the room, including Chance, looking over here." She lowered her voice. "Yes, I admit I'm in love with him, but if you all say anything…" She let the threat trail off into the sudden silence as her three friends stared at her wide-eyed.

Beth was the first one to recover, saying, "I can't believe you said the words."

"No regrets?" Zoey asked.

Tanya shook her head.

Jesse glanced toward Chance then back. "No more we're just friends?"

"Nope. I'm not gonna fight these feelings anymore. It's exhausting."

Laughter erupted from her friends, drawing everyone's attention.

"Shh. You can't say anything until I've said something to Chance." Tanya stared each of her friends directly in the eye.

After they agreed, Jesse sighed. "Of all the

times Darcy can't be here. She'll be so upset she wasn't. I can say something to her, can't I?"

"Fine." Tanya's neck tingled. Peering over her shoulder, she caught Chance studying her.

"Thankfully Alexa is all right. I know how it can be when one of your children, especially a baby, spikes a fever," Zoey said.

"I'm glad she called to let us know or I would have worried all night."

Tanya heard Jesse's comment that led to a discussion of children's illnesses, but her friends' voices slowly faded from her consciousness. From across the room all she could focus on was Chance looking at her as though no one else existed. They were the only two people in the room filled with over twenty guests.

Chance smiled, his dimples showing.

She returned his smile, then said to the group, "Excuse me."

Chance left the men and walked toward her. They met in the middle of the living room with people all around them. But the others didn't really register on her brain. Every sense fixated on the man before her, looking so incredibly handsome. The faint scent of the outdoors, from when he had helped Nick bring in the wood for the fire, clung to him.

"Hi, are you enjoying yourself?" Tanya

asked, wanting every second of the holiday season to be perfect for Chance, especially in light of her discovery that she loved him.

"Yes, how about you?" His eyes twinkled with merriment.

"Yes," she murmured as though she were a teenage girl again and dating for the first time. She was beginning to understand what Crystal was going through with her feelings for Grant Foster. "Good friends and good food. What more can you ask for?"

He took her hand and tugged her out of the path to the food table to a more secluded spot off to the side. "I want to thank you."

Every nerve ending in her hand responded to his fingers closed about hers. For a few seconds she couldn't put two coherent words together to reply to his statement. "Why?"

"I know you have gone out of your way to make sure I am included in your holiday activities as well as others."

"Am I that transparent?" She worried that she wore her feelings on her face. Did he see her love for him?

"Yep. I haven't had much downtime in the past month."

"Have I worn you out?"

"No way. Bring it on. I can keep up with you."

"Well, we need to leave for church in a while. I'm in charge of the birthday party."

A question entered Chance's eyes. "Birthday party?"

"Jesus's. After the service this evening, we have cake and punch to celebrate Christ's birth. I want to lay everything out before the service so I don't have to leave during it."

"I like that."

"What? My superb organizational skills or the celebration."

The humor in his eyes brightened. "Both actually. Are we picking up Crystal at Amanda's beforehand?"

"Yeah, Amanda's coming to church with us. Her parents will come later." Their discussion underscored how meshed their lives had become—almost as though they were a couple talking about their daughter, their plans as a family. *I want that. I want what my friends have, a husband to complete my family.*

"We'd better say our goodbyes. With the roads still snow covered it might take us longer to get to church." He placed his hand at the small of her back and guided her toward Jesse.

After they thanked Jesse for inviting them, Tanya started for the front door. In the large foyer she paused while Chance retrieved their coats from the bedroom. He assisted her into her wool wrap, then swung her around to face him. He pointed upward, his look full of mischief.

She tilted her head and saw the mistletoe with a red bow. Leave it to the town matchmaker to have mistletoe in her foyer, Tanya thought with a laugh. "Do you have something in mind, sir?"

"One or two things come to mind." He leaned forward, framing her face with his large hands. "We can't go against tradition," he whispered right before kissing her.

His mouth claimed hers in a union that rocked her to her core. His hands fell away from her cheeks, and he fit her against him, his arms trapping her in the very place she wanted to be—his embrace.

When they parted, his forehead touching hers, he murmured, "I couldn't resist. I haven't seen mistletoe in years since…" Suddenly his arms about her tensed and he straightened, pulling slightly away.

She wasn't going to let him retreat. "Since when?"

A wistful look entered his eyes. "Since the last Christmas I spent with my family. Haley had wanted to buy some when we bought the tree.

She was eleven and into boys. I think she had visions of kissing a boy under the mistletoe."

Having seen her photo in Chance's apartment, Tanya knew how pretty his daughter had been. "And you got some?" she asked in mock horror, desperate to lighten the mood.

He grinned, relaxing. "I was a sucker for her smile, but I also knew I wouldn't let a boy within ten yards of her and the mistletoe."

"Now that's the picture I see of you and your daughter."

He quirked a brow. "Tyrant and princess?"

"Yep."

His chuckle filled the air. "C'mon. Let's get Crystal and Amanda and get to church."

Hearing him say those words put a spring in her step as she and Chance made their way to her van. Bundled up against the cold night, she slipped into the passenger seat and he got behind the wheel. He'd been driving more and more. She expected him to buy a used car soon. She knew he had been saving his money. It wouldn't be long before he would have a good down payment for one.

"Mom! Mom! Time to get up."

Tanya buried herself under the blankets. She didn't want to get up even though it was Christmas morning. They hadn't gotten home from church until after one, then she hadn't been able to go to sleep for hours, thinking of her tenant. She'd wrapped Chance's presents, excitement building, making sleep impossible.

The door opened. "Mom! It's past nine. We usually have our gifts opened by now."

Tanya peeped out of the mound of covers and saw the dim light in her bedroom. "It seems like dawn."

"That's because it's snowing again."

Tanya struggled to sit up, the pull to lie back down strong. "It is? I thought it was clouding up last night when we got home."

"Yep. Big flakes. I went out on the deck for a few minutes until I got too cold."

She smiled at her daughter. "You just can't resist snow."

"Nope. C'mon, sleepyhead. I told Chance to be over in half an hour. That I'd have you up and going by then."

"You've seen him this morning?" Half an hour? Running her hands through her messy hair, Tanya scooted to the edge of her bed. Her heart already began to pound in anticipation of seeing him again in such a short time.

"He was drinking coffee on his step and enjoying the snow so he came over to keep me company while I was on the deck. He likes snow like you and I do." She turned her wheelchair around and headed out into the hall. "I promised him I would wait until he could join us to open my presents."

The second her daughter disappeared down the hall Tanya flew into action, amazed her body could move so fast when only a few minutes ago sleep weighed her limbs down. Motivation was a powerful mover. She didn't have much time, and she wanted to look her best today for Chance. She'd decided she would tell him how important he was to her. Now all she had to do was find the perfect time today.

Half an hour later she stood before her full-length mirror analyzing how she looked. With her body trimmer since she started jogging with Chance, she fit easily into last year's holiday outfit of red slacks, white lace blouse and Christmas sweater with decorated trees. Her short brown hair, still a little damp from her shower, framed her face in wisps. She moved to the mirror and put red lipstick on as the final touch.

The sound of the doorbell echoed through the house. Strange. Chance usually came to the back door, and Crystal knew that and would be waiting for him. Tanya left her room and hurried toward the front, anxious to see Chance.

When she opened the door and found Nick standing on her porch with a huge box behind him, she had to snap her mouth closed at her surprise. "What are you doing here?"

He grinned. "Making a delivery for Chance. Is he here yet?"

"I'm right here."

Tanya gasped and whirled around, her hand going to her mouth. "How did you get in here?"

"The usual way, through the back door. Crystal let me in."

"I know I'm used to the cold and everything being from Chicago, but just in case you didn't notice, it is snowing and it's Christmas morning. I promised my family I would only be gone a few minutes." Nick shifted to get hold of one side of the box with a big red bow on it.

Chance walked past Tanya and got the other side. "How did you get it to the porch?"

"Nate. He's waiting in the car. I think he thinks if he waits in the car I won't stay long."

"Clever boy," Chance said, looking toward Nick's SUV. "Tell him thanks for me."

Chance backed through the door while Tanya stepped to the side, shivering in the cold. Peering outside, she noticed the snow falling more heavily.

"Take it in the living room, then Nick, you'd

better get on home. It's getting worse." Tanya closed the door to shut out the frigid air and followed the men.

After they set the gift in front of the fireplace next to Charlie, Nick said his goodbyes and left. Tanya along with Crystal stared at the box wrapped in gold paper.

"You must have used several rolls of wrapping paper." Tanya circled the present. "Who's it for?"

"Crystal."

"Me?" Her daughter wheeled close and stopped next to it, fingering the gold paper. "This isn't one of those presents you open and there's another smaller box inside, then another one and another one?"

Chance chuckled. "No. This is a huge present."

"But I can't think of anything—"

"Open it, honey, before your mother dies of curiosity." Tanya moved to Chance's side, seeing the excitement in his expression.

The excitement was contagious as her daughter peeled off one strip of wrapping paper. It built as each piece of the box was revealed. But when the gift was finally un-wrapped, a brown box with no writing on it still kept the present hidden.

Chance shifted from one foot to the other.

"Do you want me to help with the box? I've got my pocketknife." He retrieved it and flipped it open.

"Yes, please." Crystal patted Charlie while she waited.

Chance slit the top open. Her daughter maneuvered close and stretched to see inside at the same time she did. The sight of the sports wheelchair took Tanya's breath away. She glanced back at Chance who had stepped away to let them look. His expression radiated with a bright smile.

Words congealed in her throat. She knew how expensive the wheelchair was. This was what he had been saving for—not a used car. "Chance?" was all she managed to say as she looked at Crystal, stunned, her fingers pressed to her flushed cheeks while her mouth hung open.

Silence ruled.

"What do you think? Can you use it?" Chance finally asked.

Tears welled in her daughter's eyes as she swung around to stare at Chance. One after another slipped down her face, setting off Tanya's own tears.

Crystal gestured toward the gift. "I—I—"

She swallowed several times. "I love it! It's perfect. But you shouldn't—"

Chance held up his hand. "Don't say it. The joy I see on your face is the best present I could receive. I want you to be able to play basketball and whatever else you want to that requires that kind of wheelchair."

The pressure in Tanya's chest made breathing difficult. She swiped at her tears and thought of the sacrifice this man had made for her daughter. The love she felt doubled in that instant.

"Let me get it out for you. Do you want to try it out?" He stepped to the box.

Crystal nodded while she wiped her own tears away, a huge smile on her face as she watched Chance lift it up and then place it beside Crystal's electric wheelchair. He leaned over her daughter who put her arms around his neck. He picked her up and transferred her to the shiny chrome and black sports chair, much lighter than her other one, with big wheels that were set at a slant.

Before he straightened, Crystal kissed his cheek. "Thank you doesn't seem enough."

Red patches colored his face. "That's plenty."

His roughened voice underscored how affected he was by her daughter's appreciation. Tanya kissed him on the other cheek. "Thank you. We will remember this Christmas for a long time."

He glanced at her, his dark blue gaze capturing hers. "So will I."

For a long moment no one said anything. Tanya continued to stare into his eyes, drowning in his regard that from the beginning had always made her feel so special, so womanly.

"Hey, we have other presents to open, you two."

Crystal's statement broke the connection between her and Chance. He looked away. She peered at her daughter wheeling the new chair around the living room.

"Yes, we have a gift, or rather *gifts*, for you." Tanya forced herself to step away from him and knelt by the tree to retrieve a bright package with red and green ornaments on it. "Here, open this first."

Chance sat on the couch and shook it. "It doesn't rattle." He squeezed it next. "It gives a little. A big book?"

Tanya laughed. "Open it and find out."

He tore into the wrapping and had it removed in seconds. When he saw the gift and opened to the first page of the sketchbook, he sucked in a deep breath. As he slowly flipped through the sketches, his hand trembled. "You *both* drew these," he said in awe.

Tanya eased down next to him. "We wanted you to remember this holiday and we didn't think a camera would do it justice so we drew different pictures to convey the things you did with us."

He paused and ran his finger over the pen-and-ink drawing of them decorating the four-foot tree only a few feet away. "I will cherish this always." His voice thickened with each word he said.

"Good. It wasn't easy because these sketches are big, but we made a copy of them for ourselves. We don't want to forget this Christmas, either." Crystal did a tight circle in her new chair.

Chance closed his hand over Tanya's, and her pulse rate soared. "Your presence has been such a nice treat for us."

She didn't tell him that both her and her daughter felt as if this holiday was a new beginning for them—the past finally behind them. They had loved Tom and mourned his loss, but they needed to move forward. Crystal's accident, Tom's conviction and ultimately his death in prison had shaped so much of the past four years. Her daughter deserved more—a life as normal as possible. She prayed one day that he could move forward, the past behind him, too.

Chance shifted so he could face her on the couch. "I could say the same for you two. I'm the grateful one getting to share in your Christmas celebration."

When Crystal wheeled herself into the kitchen, Tanya sandwiched his hand between hers. "You shouldn't have spent so much. I know those chairs are expensive. You were supposed to be getting yourself a car."

His grin reached deep into his eyes. "I will, just later. I like to walk."

"But it's snowing, has been a lot these past few weeks."

"The cold is invigorating to me. I like to walk in the snow. After dinner let's go for a walk."

"I've got another gift for you." She released his hand and hurried to the tree, getting the second present—the most important one. Back at his side, she laid it in his lap.

He hefted it up. "This I know has got to be a book." Again he ripped the silver wrapping paper off quickly to reveal a black Bible with his name engraved in gold on the front at the bottom right hand corner. He touched the lettering then slanted a look at her. "Thank you, Tanya. This means a lot to me. One of the things I wish I hadn't lost was my family Bible. Now I have a new one."

When she had first met him and realized how he had felt about God, she hadn't thought she would hear him say something like that. But he had found his way back to the Lord. That was the best gift she could have received the whole season. "I have marked a few places you might want to read."

Tanya heard Crystal opening and closing a cabinet door, probably searching for something to eat. "I'd better get the prime rib in the oven if we're gonna have dinner at a reasonable hour." She started to rise.

He stopped her. "First, I want to give you your present."

"Me? But you've already spent too much on Crystal."

"Did you think I would neglect to give you something to remember me by?"

Her heart slammed into her ribs. The way he'd phrased the question made it seem as if he was leaving Sweetwater soon. She supposed after the New Year was soon. Before she could say anything, he held out a long, thin box in his palm. She stared at the gold-wrapped present.

Can't he see Sweetwater is perfect for him? That I am? Lord, that's all the gift I need. For him to return to Sweetwater after the trial.

"Aren't you gonna open it?"

She blinked, willing the hammering of her heart to slow. He might not have really meant he was leaving for good. *Perhaps he sees how good this town is for him.* "Of course." Slowly she took it from him but not before he clasped her fingers and tugged her to him, kissing her, quick and hard.

She carefully unwrapped the present and lifted the lid. Beneath some tissue lay a beautiful gold chain with an outline of a heart dangling from it with a diamond sparkling in its right corner. She held up the necklace, the gem gleaming. "It's beautiful."

"When I saw it in the store, I immediately knew it was perfect for you. You have such a good heart. You're so caring of others."

The swelling in her throat captured her words. All she could do was hand him the chain and turn so he could hook the necklace around her neck. The feel of his fingers on her nape sent tingles down her spine. She squeezed her eyes closed and imagined they were a real family, celebrating Christmas.

"There," he whispered close to her ear, his lips brushing her lobe.

She melted back against him, weak with wanting him. His hands clasped her upper arms, his breath feathering her neck. She turned her head to the side, and he planted tiny kisses along her jaw.

"Don't let anyone ever tell you otherwise, Tanya. You're a beautiful, loving woman who deserves the very best."

Even though he said all the right words, she felt as if there was a "but" at the end of the last sentence. She twisted around to face him, trying to read his expression which suddenly blanked. "What are you trying to tell me?"

"The truth as I see it. Those sketches you did for me were great. Share your talent with others. Look what it has done for Crystal. Let people see what you're capable of."

Again she sensed something left unsaid but realized Chance wouldn't expound on it unless he wanted to. "I'll think about it."

He stared long and hard into her eyes, then rose and offered her his hand. "Let's put that roast in the oven. I'll help you."

He pulled her to her feet, then headed to the kitchen. Crystal sat at the table, drinking some milk and eating a bowl of cereal.

When her daughter saw them, she said, "I'm gonna have to lift weights to build up the muscles more in my arms."

"You can use the weight room at the center

to get started." Chance planted himself at the counter, lounging back against it.

"Yeah. I'd been thinking about it anyway, and now with this chair, I have to if I want to play sports and be any good."

"Besides basketball, what are you thinking about?" Tanya removed the prime rib from the refrigerator.

"There's track-and-field events. I could do some racing."

As Crystal and Chance discussed the possibilities open for her daughter, Tanya prepared the roast and stuck it into the oven. With all that had happened this morning she was even more determined to tell him how she felt about him. Then if he still left, at least he would have all the facts. She wanted no regrets when it came to him.

Tanya matched her strides with Chance's as she strode beside him later Christmas Day. Crystal had urged them to go for a walk while she talked with her friends on the phone, no doubt comparing presents.

The snow continued to fall but lightly now. The clouds cast the sky in different hues of gray. The scent of burning wood laced the crisp winter air. The snow blanketed the terrain in pristine white, undisturbed in most places as the majority of the townspeople stayed indoors.

"I think a lot of people miss the beauty of winter holed up in their houses." Tanya swept her arm across her body to indicate the area before them.

"I agree, but then it wouldn't be as beautiful if they were all trampling through the snow."

"Like us? So you think we should keep this a secret from them?"

"Yep. It's here if they want to partake of its beauty."

Tanya laughed. "That's kinda hard when some have pulled their drapes already." She pointed toward the house they were passing.

"Yeah, it's only four. We have another hour of daylight." He cut down another street and headed for the lake.

"And the ones who see us walking are probably thinking we're crazy for being out here."

At the lake the water appeared dark gray-blue and icy. With no wind blowing its surface was mirror smooth. Tall pines, the only green in the landscape, skirted the shoreline, poking themselves up out of the white cover of snow. Tanya paused at the edge and stared across the lake. She needed to tell Chance her feelings, but for the life of her she didn't know where to begin.

Lord, help me to say the right words. I feel as if my tongue has swollen in my dry mouth all of a sudden.

The large boulder she had often used to sit on by the water beckoned. Tanya dusted the snow off its surface and sat. Chance stood in front of her wearing his heavy black coat with no gloves or cap.

"You aren't cold?" Tanya touched her red hat that kept her ears warm.

"Nah. The cold makes me feel alive. In winter we didn't get outside as much so I enjoy any time I can be outdoors."

Tell him. "Your ears are red."

"They'll survive. A few minutes in front of your fire and they'll be toasty warm."

"Do you have a busy week at work?"

"No, Nick let a lot of people off because of the holidays. I've got a project I need to finish up, but that's all."

She glanced at the water lapping gently against the shore, the only sound in the quiet. "You know what I miss the most during the winter is the animals, especially the birds. We have a few, but most of them go south for the winter." *Tell him!*

At that moment a red cardinal left his perch on a branch of an oak tree that still retained its brown leaves. She followed his flight for a minute before looking back at Chance. The regret in his eyes stole her breath. He lowered his lashes and veiled it.

"When are you leaving?" she blurted out the question without really thinking.

His sharp intake of air filled the silence. "The trial starts in less than two weeks."

Will you be back afterward? she wanted to ask but was afraid of the answer. Instead she pushed herself off the large rock, positioning herself only a few feet from him. "You aren't alone, Chance. God is with you."

"I know. There's a part of me that doesn't want to go to the trial."

"Then don't. If you're testifying only go for that part."

His intense gaze riveted to hers. "I have to go. I want to say goodbye and this is my chance to do that."

"God's not the only one with you. I am, too."

"I know. You're a good friend." His intensity faded.

Tell him. "I want to be more than a friend, Chance. I've fallen in love with you."

His eyes widened. He dropped his gaze, twisting around to stare at the lake. "You shouldn't have, Tanya. I'm not free to love."

His past continued to haunt him, holding him prisoner as if he were still in prison. His rigid stance conveyed the barrier that might always be between them. For the first time since she'd begun the walk, cold seeped in, straight to the marrow of her bones, leaving her frozen with despair.

Chapter Twelve

Blessed be the God and Father of our Lord Jesus Christ, which according to His abundant mercy hath begotten us again unto a lively hope by the resurrection of Jesus Christ from the dead. The words from Peter, that Samuel had quoted in his sermon, leaped off the page, entwining themselves into Chance's heart. Christ offered him hope—hope that one day he could have a life rid of this guilt that ate into his soul.

Closing the Bible that Tanya had given him, Chance rose and walked to the window. The sound of the basketball striking against the concrete then the backboard drew him. He watched Crystal take another shot at the hoop. When the ball bounced off the rim and landed in the grass alongside the driveway, Charlie went after it and nosed it toward Crystal. She dribbled then set up for another shot. Chance turned toward the door.

He had avoided Tanya all week since Christmas day and her declaration of love. She deserved to be loved by someone who could come to her with a clear heart—not him. And above all, she deserved to know the whole story about him and Tom before he left for Louisville.

His hand on the knob, Chance rested his forehead against the wood. He loved her. But he wasn't free to love Tanya as she should be. Hate and guilt crowded his heart. How could he enter into a relationship she deserved when he couldn't straighten out his own life? She had endured so much these past few years. He would never forgive himself if he added to her pain.

Once he told her he was the reason Tom was killed, her love would die and he could leave. Turning the knob, he opened the door and stepped outside onto the landing.

The basketball slamming into the driveway over and over echoed in the air. He descended the stairs.

When Crystal saw him, she smiled and cradled the ball in her lap. Although the temperature was only in the low fifties, beads of sweat pebbled her forehead. She swiped the back of her hand across her forehead.

"This is hard work, but since the snow melted yesterday, I've got to grab the chance to practice while I have it." She lined up the ball toward the hoop and sent it flying. It swished through the net. "Yes!"

Chance loped toward the ball as it hit the concrete and caught it before it bounced a second time. He tossed it toward Crystal who trapped it against her body.

"You've done a good job teaching Charlie to help retrieve your ball."

She called her service dog to her and stroked the length of his back. "He's always been a quick learner." With the ball in her lap, she rolled toward the deck ramp.

When Chance saw Crystal struggling up the ramp, easily accessible for an electric wheelchair, he started toward her but stopped. He gave her a few more seconds to see if she would make it on her own. That was important to Crystal. When she reached the top of the ramp, she swung around, her grin wide.

"I started working out at the center. Before long going up this ramp will be a piece of cake."

"Your arms have to be tired. You've been practicing for the past hour."

"Yep. I hear we might have another round of snow next week. You would think we live in Alaska the way it has been snowing this past month."

Chance took a wooden lounge chair opposite Crystal. "Have you played any basketball at the center yet?"

"Not yet. I will when I get better. I'm thinking in the spring of joining a wheelchair basketball team that's part of a league that meets in Lexington. Mom said she would drive me to the practices and the games." She leaned forward. "Thank you again for this chair. I've always loved sports, and now I can participate in them more."

Chance glanced toward the back door and wondered where Tanya was. He really needed to talk to her, but he realized sitting with Crystal was his way of avoiding what he must do. He didn't want to see the pain, disappointment and anger in Tanya's face. But it was better this way. A quick sever would be less painful than a prolonged one.

"Have you decided on what sports besides basketball that you want to do? I know you mentioned track and field once."

"I've been researching some different ones online and I think racing would be the best one for me. Also, I'm gonna talk with Darcy about getting more involved with riding."

"Your mom told me you've gotten back up on a horse since your accident, but you aren't riding like you used to."

"I want to again. I don't blame the horse for my paralysis." She stared down at her lap for a good minute then lifted her gaze toward him. "Blame is such negative energy. I've decided I don't have room for that in my life. I used to blame myself for what my father did."

"But you weren't at fault."

"I know that now. I prayed a lot about it, especially after he died. For a time I thought I had killed him."

No, I did. Chance clenched his teeth, unable to say the words.

Crystal sought Charlie, who laid his head in her lap. She scratched him behind his ear. "Guilt is like blame. It's negative energy. It doesn't do any good for a person. If God can forgive me, then why shouldn't I forgive myself?"

"It's not always that easy," Chance murmured, thinking of his own guilt that he carried around.

"'But if we walk in the light, as He is in the light, we have fellowship one with another, and the blood of Jesus Christ His Son cleanseth us from all sin.' I remember Samuel telling me that one day last summer and it all made sense."

The creak of the back door opening sounded. Chance glanced toward Tanya. A piercing pain knifed through his heart. He was going to hurt her. There was no way around it. The idea cut him deeply.

For a few seconds while he and Tanya stared at each other, he thought about fleeing as far from Sweetwater as he could get. And he would. But first he had to tell her everything concerning Tom.

"Hi, Mom. Did you see me shooting? I made a couple of baskets. Before long, Chance, I'm gonna have you raise the basket to regulation height."

He stood. "It's easy. Anyone can for you."

Crystal gave him a questioning look but didn't say anything. Instead, she rolled her chair into the house while Tanya held the door open. He followed, his throat jammed with emotions of regret and a much more intense feeling he wished he could deny.

"I need to clean up. Tonight is New Year's Eve and I've got a feeling this next year is gonna be a good one so I want to be up to greet it."

"Do you hear her?" Tanya stood in the middle of the kitchen watching her daughter disappear into the hallway. "She is happy." She swung around to face him. "And part of the reason for that is you, Chance."

"If that is so, then I've accomplished one of the thing I wanted to do when I came to Sweetwater."

Confusion created deep creases in her brow. "What do you mean?"

Lord, I need Your help. How do I tell Tanya without hurting her? But nothing came to Chance's mind as he stared at the woman who had come to mean so much to him. He sucked in a deep, fortifying breath then released it slowly. "It wasn't Samuel who brought me to Sweetwater. It was you."

"Me? But you didn't even know me."

"Yes, I did. Tom often talked about you and Crystal. We had a lot of downtime while in prison and he would tell me different stories."

"What did he say?" Curiosity replaced her puzzlement.

"I heard about your vacation to the Smoky Mountains. I heard about the baby squirrel Crystal found and raised until it was big enough to live on its own. Through all the stories I heard the love he had for you and Crystal. He told me right before he died that he regretted everything he had done to you two. He didn't understand your manic depression, but he thought you were a loving, caring woman. He didn't understand how God could have allowed something like Crystal's paralysis to happen to her. Toward the end he was filled with hopelessness and bitterness, but he always loved you two."

Tanya spun around and took two steps to the table to settle onto a chair. Her hand shook as she smoothed back her hair. "I still don't understand why he thought he had to go it alone. He would have gotten out of prison, and we could have been a family again."

"I think in his mind he thought his life was over." The pounding in his chest echoed in his ears. If he didn't say something now, he might never. "I'm the reason Tom was killed."

Lifting her head, she looked at him. "You? I don't understand."

"A couple of inmates had me cornered and were intent on killing me. Tom stepped in and took the knife meant for me. I had had enough of being pushed around and had stood up to the wrong person. Tom was killed because of me."

She blinked.

A long silence fell between them.

Finally she rose, slowly. "Why didn't you tell me before?"

"I wanted to help you and Crystal, and I didn't think you would let me if you knew."

"So you kept it a secret!" Tears glinted in her eyes as she stepped toward him, her hands clenched at her sides.

"Yes."

"Why say anything now?"

"I wasn't gonna say anything to you, but you deserve to know everything."

"So Crystal and I were a charity case for you, and now that you've done what you set out to do, you're ready to leave." Anger sliced through her words.

"Yes," he said, even though she hadn't asked a question. The thunderous beat of his heart continued to vibrate through his mind. "I have unfinished business in Louisville."

"And afterward?" Steel strengthened her voice.

"I don't know. I can't think beyond the trial."

Her usual expressive face evolved into a neutral facade. She walked to the back door and opened it. "Thanks for letting me know about how Tom really died."

He strode toward her, wanting so badly to take her into his arms and hug her until her anger melted. When he came alongside her, her words stopped him.

"And you don't need to worry about Crystal and me. We're doing just fine, and don't need any more of your help."

"Tanya," he started but couldn't find the words to express his feelings. He still had to deal with his past and put to rest the guilt and anger that choked him when he thought about the murder of his family. He wouldn't involve Tanya in that. She'd been through enough. "Happy New Year," he murmured finally and left.

Outside on the deck he flinched at the sound of the door slamming behind him. Glancing around at the shadows of dusk creeping over the yard, he knew what he needed to do next. He couldn't stay until the start of the trial. He needed to leave now. A clean break was best for Tanya, and he'd already hurt her enough today. He didn't want to cause her any more pain by lingering a few extra days. He strode across the driveway to the stairs that led to his apartment.

Tanya watched Chance head for the apartment above the garage. Numbing shock gripped her in a tight vise. Tom died trying to break up a fight between Chance and two other inmates. Her emotions lay frozen within her. She didn't know what to feel.

There had been no future for her and Tom for years. Ever since he had set fire to the first barn, their future had been sealed in her husband's mind. But even before that, there had been a rift in their relationship partly due to the fact he hadn't been understanding about her manic depression. She had struggled alone dealing with it, and it had taken a toll on her marriage that Crystal's accident had completely torn apart.

Tanya turned away from the window and made her way toward her bedroom and lay on her bed, staring at the ceiling. Darkness slithered into the room, and she welcomed it as she willed her mind empty of any thoughts. But on the black screen of her mind all she could see was Chance, the pain in his eyes when he had looked at her the last time before leaving her house. She wasn't even sure he was aware of his expression.

But she was sure of one thing: she had moved on in her life. She no longer felt guilty about Tom. And she was no longer angry at Tom for what he had done to their lives, to his life.

Finally she sat up and swung her legs over the edge of the bed. After switching on the lamp on her bedside table, she pulled her Bible onto her lap and opened it, searching for peace in its pages.

Dawn broke on the horizon. Tanya saw the streaks of red-orange entwined through the dark blue and wished she had some answers to the hundreds of questions that had plagued her through the night. The overriding one, what did she do now, still demanded an answer she didn't have.

The scent of perking coffee drifted to her, and she walked to the pot to pour herself a huge mugful. The gritty feel in her eyes reminded her of the sleepless night that had passed. Some time in the middle of the night she had closed her Bible. Peace had eluded her, but the need to see Chance had grown as she had read the Word.

Sipping the brew, she stared out the window at the stairs to Chance's apartment. She loved him and realized that hadn't changed even with the new information she had learned the day before.

Was she going to allow Tom to continue to dictate how she lived her life? He had chosen his path, even when he had stepped in front of the knife meant for Chance. Tom's death wasn't Chance's fault.

But Chance felt it was. Could she find a way to make him understand it wasn't? Even if Chance didn't love her, he deserved to forgive himself for what happened to Tom. That was the least she could give Chance. Peace of mind. Then maybe she would have her own peace.

Still dressed in her jeans and sweatshirt from

the day before, she took one last swig of her coffee, placed it on the counter and strode to the back door. Outside the crisp winter air chilled her. She hurried toward the stairs that led to his place. She took them two at a time and started to knock when she noticed the door wasn't totally shut.

He was gone! She knew it in her heart. Her hands quivered as she opened the door and entered the apartment. Scanning the large room through a sheen of tears she saw that every trace of Chance was wiped away. Her gaze rested on the kitchen table where a note propped next to a wad of money sat. Slowly she crossed to it and reached for the paper with her name on it.

Her hand clutched it as she read the short letter.

Tanya, the time spent with you and Crystal has been wonderful. I have left you this month's rent as my notice. May you find a man who one day deserves your goodness. Love, Chance.

Love, Chance. Did that mean he loved her? Was that just a casual closing to his note that really meant nothing? Frustration at no answers churned in her stomach.

She crumpled the letter into a ball and threw it across the room. Anger consumed her. How dare he leave without saying goodbye in person! How dare— Then she remembered the last time she had seen him, yesterday when confusion reigned in her. She couldn't blame him. She had basically kicked him out of her house.

She collapsed onto a chair and buried her face in her palms. She'd made a mess of the situation. And now Chance was gone. She had no idea where he was, at least not until the trial started next week.

Chance stood at the window of his hotel room, glimpsing the Ohio River in the distance. The gray day reflected his mood. The first day of the trial had gone smoothly with the selection of the jurors in the morning and the opening remarks in the afternoon. He'd held up, even through the attorneys' remarks to the jury, mostly by shutting down his emotions totally and staring a hole in the back of the chair in front of him. He'd barely gotten out of there before all his feelings had inundated him.

Gripping the window ledge, he leaned his forehead against the cold pane. Icy fingers spread through him, cooling the heat of his anger. The man who had destroyed his life had sat next to his lawyer, smug, unaffected by the trial.

Lord, I can't do this!

Even though the trial wasn't expected to last long, he didn't know how he was going to make in through all the testimony day in and day out. Flashes of his past blinked in and out of his mind—finding his family murdered, being charged with those murders, the years spent in prison knowing he was innocent and the real killer was walking free, something he never thought he would do again.

God, help me! I have to do this much for Ruth and Haley, see this trial through to the end. I owe them that.

A knock sounded at the door. He spun around and stared at it as though he hadn't really heard anything.

Another rap filled the silence.

As though his legs had a will of their own, they carried him across the room. He reached for the handle in slow motion and pulled the door open. When he saw Tanya before him, he nearly fell apart. Her inner beauty shone from her eyes, her smile of greeting melting the icy shroud that blanketed him.

Time faded away as he stared at her here in

the hallway outside his hotel room, not in Sweetwater where she belonged.

Finally one of her delicate brows rose. "Can I come in?"

"How did you find me?"

"Nick helped me. He figured you would be staying near the courthouse. I wish I could have been here yesterday, but I had to work in order to get the rest of the week off."

"The rest of the week?"

She peeked around him. "Let's talk in your room."

"Oh," he said, realizing he still blocked the entrance. He stepped to the side to allow her inside.

"I'm here to support you through the trial." Tanya turned in the middle of the room to face him.

"Why?"

"Because no one should have to go through what you're going through alone. You need your...friends. Nick and the rest of them are coming tomorrow."

"But..." He didn't know what to say. "Everyone?"

"Yep."

"Why would—"

Tanya covered the space between them in

two quick strides. She placed her fingers against his mouth to still his words. "Whether you want to admit it or not, you have a lot of people in Sweetwater who care about you and don't want you to go through the trial alone so there's nothing you can do but put up with us."

The feel of her fingers pressing into his lips, the look of love in her eyes, released the dam on his emotions. They flooded him, rendering him humble in the power of the Lord. Tanya was here because God had sent her. She had been there all along for him, but he hadn't wanted to see it, had fought it all the way.

Chance gathered Tanya to him, burying his face in her hair, the apple-scented shampoo she used washing over him. Tears crowded his eyes. He squeezed them closed, holding them inside, but they clogged his throat, making any comments impossible.

Minutes later he finally pulled back, keeping his arms loosely about her. He swallowed several times before he was able to ask, "You took vacation days to be here?"

She nodded. Lifting her hand, she cupped his jaw. The sheen in her eyes indicated the depth of her feelings for him. They humbled him anew. How in the world did he deserve someone like Tanya?

The question put some emotional distance between him and Tanya. There was so much baggage that stood in the way of having any kind of future together.

Tanya must have sensed his thoughts because a cloud masked the joy in her gaze. "We have a lot to talk about, but first you need to get through the trial. The rest can come later."

"I wish it were that easy."

"It won't be easy. I never said that. But you need to let me help you as you helped me. Lo— friendship is a two-way street." Tanya slipped her fingers from his face. "What time do we need to be at the courthouse?"

"Nine."

"Then we'd better get moving. But first let's pray." Tanya took both his hands and bowed her head. "Dear Heavenly Father, watch over Chance in his time of need. Help to ease his pain and pave the way for him to forgive the man who took his family. In Jesus Christ's name, amen."

Chance yanked his hands free. "Forgive! How can you expect me to forgive that man after all he did to me and my family?"

"Because until you do, you won't be totally free to move on. He will pay for his crimes, but I don't want to see you continue to pay because you can't forgive him."

He spun around. "I don't think I can. We'd better get going. I don't want to be late."

Hopefully it will be over tomorrow, Chance thought by Thursday evening after spending the whole week in the courtroom. The jury was deliberating as he sat in his darkened hotel room. He didn't think they would be out long because the evidence had been compelling. But then a jury had convicted him on circumstantial evidence that had thrown his already messed-up life into a tailspin so it was hard to tell what a jury would do.

Only in the past few days with first Tanya and later her circle of friends and their husbands sitting around him as support had he experienced again the peace he had felt that time in church with Tanya. He could still feel the comfort of her hand within his throughout the closing statements by each of the lawyers. Each look, touch had soothed his pain until now all he wanted to do was let go of this anger that had consumed him for years while he had sat in a cell—imprisoned physically, and as he knew now, mentally, too.

Lord, I don't want to feel this way anymore. What do I do?

In the dark he caught sight of his Bible on the

table in front of the window, a stream of light illuminating it. Every night before going to sleep he had read it until his eyes had drooped closed.

He flipped on the lamp beside him and reached for his Bible. Tanya had insisted he had to forgive his family's killer in order to be totally at peace and able to move on. *How do I do that, Father?*

He turned to Luke and read the account of Christ's ministry, his death. "Then said Jesus, 'Father, forgive them; for they know not what they do.' And they parted his raiment, and cast lots."

The words leaped off the page, striking Chance with their meaning. *If Christ can forgive the people who tormented and killed him, then the least I can do is the same: forgive the man who murdered my wife and daughter.*

After finishing Luke, Chance closed his Bible and fingered the gold letters of his name engraved in the black cover.

He imagined the killer in his mind. "I forgive you," he whispered into the silence of the room. Then in a stronger voice he repeated, "I forgive you."

With each word uttered, a part of his anger dissolved. Left in its wake was the peace he had craved.

* * *

Tightening her grasp on his hand, Tanya slid a glance toward Chance as the verdict was read. His somber expression evolved into relief as the word "guilty" was spoken in the quiet courtroom. The taut line of his shoulders sagged and he dropped his head, his eyes closing for a few seconds.

"It's over," he whispered to her, his voice raw.

Tanya released his hand and opened her arms to him. He went into her embrace. His shudder passed through his body and into hers.

"I'm finally free. Really free."

Around them people stood, talked, moved about, but Tanya sat in the front row with Chance and held him for minutes. When he pulled back, she saw a new man in his eyes, a man who had closed the door on his past and faced his future with hope. Joy spread through her.

Her arms fell away. She smiled. "Justice was finally done today."

"Yes, Gary Kingston has to face the consequences of what he did. I hope he finds some kind of peace over it."

This was the first time Chance had said the man's name out loud to her. He'd always used "murderer" or "killer" before this. "You do?"

He nodded. "I had to forgive him. I—"

Nick approached and sat in the vacant chair behind Chance. "We want to celebrate. Do you two feel up to dinner at the hotel before we all head back to Sweetwater?"

Tanya scanned her friends and their husbands waiting near the entrance into the now almost-empty courtroom. Even Darcy was here with her new baby to support Chance. Emotions crammed her throat at how lucky she was to have friends like Darcy, Jesse, Beth and Zoey.

"Sure. You all go ahead. I want to have a word with Tanya. We'll be along in a few minutes." Chance shook Nick's hand. "Thanks for being here."

"Anything for a friend. We'll save you a seat." Nick made his way toward his wife, slipping his arm around her shoulder as the group left.

"Let's go find a quiet place in the hall." Chance rose and held his hand out for her.

After fitting hers in his grasp, she walked beside him out into the foyer. Chance quickly found an empty bench and drew her to it. As she leaned against the hard back slats, her heart slowed. Was he going to tell her goodbye? Did he want to move on without her? Maybe he didn't love her enough to marry her. And she realized more than ever she wanted to get married again. She wanted the happiness her friends had.

Chance swallowed hard, clasping her other hand, too. "Thank you for being here with me. After that first day, I didn't know how I was going to get through the trial, then you showed up on my doorstep and gave me a way. I know about all you had to do to be here with me."

"I'd do it again."

He grinned. "I know. And I have several people back in Sweetwater to thank. Amanda's parents who agreed to take Crystal in and trade cars with you so they could transport Crystal in the van. Your boss, for letting you take time off suddenly. Not to mention all your friends who came."

"They're your friends, too."

"Until this week I hadn't really realized that. I never had friends like them. I was always working too hard to have time for other people except my family and even then I didn't spend enough time with them. I can't get that back, but I can move forward, live the type of life Christ spoke of. Learn from my mistakes."

Little creases lined his forehead as he spoke. Tanya wanted to smooth them away, but he held her hands and she loved the feel of his fingers entwined with hers.

"And the most important thing I've learned in the past few months is that I love you, Tanya. I want to spend the rest of my life with you."

One small seed of doubt nibbled at her. "You aren't saying that because of your guilt over how Tom died, are you? This isn't some kind of payback?"

He shook his head. "Tom wanted to die. He made the choice to step in between me and my attacker to take that knife. I know that now. Last night when I forgave Gary Kingston, I also forgave myself."

"I never really blamed you for Tom's death. I didn't get a chance to tell you because you left before I could. And we've been busy with the trial. I came over to see you New Year's Day early in the morning to let you know that. But you were gone. I was angry because you didn't trust me earlier with knowing the details of how Tom had died."

"I was wrong. I should have. But I had become so used to seeing people shun me that I didn't want to see that in your eyes. I realize now that I was falling in love with you and was scared to do anything to change that so I kept quiet."

"Why did you tell me then?"

A full-fledged grin returned. "Because I was in love with you and was scared to be in love again.

I used it to put distance between us, an excuse to leave you. I won't make that mistake again."

"I'll hold you to that." The joy she had held at bay burst out of its restraints and flooded her. She slipped her hands from his and drew him to her. "I love you, Chance. I want to spend the rest of my life with you."

His mouth claimed hers in a deep kiss. She relished the sensations he generated in her.

His breathing ragged, he asked, "Will you marry me?"

"Yes! Yes!"

Again he possessed her mouth with his, leaving no doubt in her mind that he loved her with all his being.

When Chance finally rose, he laced his fingers through hers and tugged her gently to her feet. "I guess we'd better not keep our friends waiting. After all, we have a lot to celebrate tonight, and if I can't have you alone, then I can't think of any better way to celebrate than with friends."

Fifteen minutes later, Tanya strode into the hotel restaurant with Chance by her side. She knew her love for the man next to her was written all over her face. That was shortly confirmed when the waiter showed them into the small room that Nick had secured for their dinner.

When her friends looked at them, one by one they rose, clapping, with smiles that matched the grins plastered on her face and Chance's.

"I don't think we need to ask what has kept you two. Care to share any news with us?" Jesse reseated herself next to her husband.

"Tanya has agreed to become my wife."

More applause and cheers followed Chance's announcement. Tanya squeezed his hand and slanted a look his way. His gaze, trained on her, flared with the promise of friendship *and* love.

"When?" Beth asked when everyone quieted.

Tanya eased into the chair that Chance held for her. "We haven't set a date, but I've always wanted a June wedding."

"A June bride! How wonderful!" Darcy patted her baby on the back. "That gives us time to really plan a beautiful wedding."

As Jesse, Beth, Zoey and Darcy began to discuss their ideas for the wedding, Chance leaned down, kissed Tanya's neck by her ear and whispered, "We can always elope. It's your call."

Epilogue

"The last item up for bidding is an opportunity to have a portrait painted by our very own Tanya Taylor. Just in case a person hasn't seen the wonderful work she does, I have a portrait here to show you." Samuel held up a picture of Beth and his children that Tanya had done for him.

The heat of a blush tinged Tanya's cheeks as she heard the admiration of her neighbors. She snuggled closer to Chance, never comfortable being in the limelight.

"You'd better get used to hearing people comment on your work. You're garnishing quite a reputation. This is bound to bring in the largest amount for the Fourth of July Auction." Grinning, Chance kissed her cheek.

"Hey, the honeymoon ended two weeks ago, you two," Zoey said next to Chance.

Tanya felt her blush deepen and spread down her neck. She and Chance had had a wonderfully planned wedding, given to her by Jesse, Darcy, Beth and Zoey, followed by a honeymoon to the Bahamas that had been Nick and Jesse's wedding present to them. The joy that had come into her life with Chance blossomed each day she spent with him.

Ten minutes later the president of the bank where she worked had indeed set a record for what one item brought in for the church's outreach program and put an end to the auction. Chance, Nick and Dane cleared off the gym floor at the center so the next part of the afternoon's activities could begin.

When Chance settled next to Tanya in the bleachers, he took her hand. "Okay?"

"Nervous."

"She'll do great. She's been practicing for months. And I don't think Crystal's minded all the practice one bit since Grant has been giving her pointers."

At that moment Crystal and the rest of her team rolled out onto the floor to give an exhibition of wheelchair basketball for the spectators. Tanya held her breath as the ball was set in motion. One of her daughter's teammates dribbled down the court, passed it to Crystal and she took a shot. It circled the rim and swished through the net.

Tanya jumped to her feet and cheered, Chance right next to her, yelling even louder than her. Through the exhibition Crystal's smile grew as the enthusiasm of the crowd grew.

At the end, Tanya threw her arms around her husband. "She is good!"

He captured her gaze. "Just like her mom." His hand cupped the back of her neck. "I never thought I would be so happy, Mrs. Taylor."

She stood on tiptoes and brushed her lips across his. "Me neither. You have brought me such joy, Mr. Taylor."

* * * * *

Dear Reader,

This was the last book in THE LADIES OF SWEETWATER LAKE series. I will miss these characters, having really gotten to know them over the course of five books. Tanya's story was the hardest one to write. She was wounded and hurting, and until Chance came into her life, didn't realize she could help another to heal.

In *Tidings of Joy,* Crystal, and to a certain extent, Chance, had to deal with a bully. I teach in a high school and have seen firsthand the harm a bully can do to another. If you or a loved one are dealing with a bully, get help. Don't try to cope on your own. If you witness a bullying situation, speak up for the person who is targeted. Bystanders can make a difference in a bullying situation.

There are some excellent books about bullying and what can be done to stop it. I had the pleasure of listening to Barbara Coloroso speak on bullying in our school. Her book, *The Bully, the Bullied, and the Bystander,* offers good suggestions to parents and teachers about making changes in how we raise our children to break the cycle of violence we've seen in our cultures and schools.

I love hearing from my readers. You can contact me at P.O. Box 2074, Tulsa OK 74101, or visit my Web site at www.margaretdaley.com, where you can sign up for my quarterly newsletter.

Margaret Daley

QUESTIONS FOR DISCUSSION

1. Tanya dealt with manic depression, an illness she would have to take medication to control. She didn't like having to depend on the medicine, but she didn't have a choice. What things have you had to do that you had no choice over? Did your faith help you deal with it? How?

2. Chance couldn't move on in his life because he couldn't forgive himself or the man responsible for his wife's and daughter's deaths. How hard is it to forgive another? Have you ever not been able to forgive? How does that affect you spiritually, emotionally?

3. Crystal was being harassed by a couple of girls at school. Have you ever been bullied? How did you deal with it? What are some things we can do to prevent bullying?

4. Crystal, and even Chance, learned to turn the other cheek against the people bothering them. When have you done this? How did it make you feel?

5. Tanya hid her talent as an artist because she feared rejection. Fear of rejection is a powerful emotion that controls our actions, as it did in Tanya's case. How has fear of rejection controlled you? How have you overcome it's hold on you?

6. Chance went to prison, even though he was innocent. He lived in a nightmarish situation for over two years. Even after he left prison, he still lived in a self-imposed one, built by guilt and the inability to forgive. Have you ever lived in a self-imposed prison? How did you move on? Did your faith play a part in breaking those bonds? How?

7. When Holly needed a tutor for math, Crystal came forward and volunteered to do it. In Romans 12:20 it states, "Therefore if thine enemy hunger, feed him; if he thirst, give him drink." That can be hard to do when you have been hurt by another. What has helped you to forgive your enemy?

8. John 14:27 says, "Peace I leave with you, my peace I give unto you: not as the world giveth, give I unto you. Let not your heart be troubled neither let it be afraid." In the end, through the Lord, Chance found the peace he had been seeking. Has this happened to you? How did you find your peace?

9. Tanya worried about her daughter—so much had happened to Crystal over the past four years. To Tanya, God and her circle of friends were the ones who had gotten her through the hard times. Who do you rely on during the tough times? How?

10. Crystal was in a wheelchair. Tanya had manic depression. We all have some kind of disability we have to cope with, whether physical, emotional or spiritual. What is yours? How do you cope? Does your faith help? How?

2 Love Inspired novels and a mystery gift... Absolutely FREE!

Visit
www.LoveInspiredBooks.com
for your two FREE books, sent directly to you!

BONUS: Choose between regular print or our NEW larger print format!

There's no catch! You're under no obligation to buy anything. We charge nothing—ZERO—for your first shipment. And you don't have to make any minimum number of purchases.

You'll like the convenience of home delivery at our special discount prices, and you'll love your free subscription to Steeple Hill News, our members-only newsletter.

We hope that after receiving your free books, you'll want to remain a subscriber. But the choice is yours— to continue or cancel, anytime at all! So why not take us up on our invitation, with no risk of any kind!